HUNTED

SELENA WINTERS

COPYRIGHT

Hunted Copyright © 2024 Selena Winters

All Rights Reserved.
No part of this publication may be reproduced, stored, or transmitted in any form or by any means, electronic, mechanical, photocopying, recording, scanning, or otherwise without written permission from the publisher. It is illegal to copy this book, post it to a website, or distribute it by any other means without permission.

This novel is entirely a work of fiction. The names, characters and incidents portrayed in it are the work of the author's imagination. Any resemblance to actual persons, living or dead, events or localities is entirely coincidental.

Warning: the unauthorized reproduction or distribution of this copyrighted work is illegal. Criminal copyright infringement, including infringement without monetary gain, is investigated by the FBI and is punishable by up to 5 years in prison and a fine of $250,000.

CONTENTS

Copyright	1
Dedication	5
Playlist	7
Author's Note	9
1. Zara	11
2. Aksel	19
3. Zara	27
4. Aksel	33
5. Zara	41
6. Aksel	45
7. Zara	53
8. Aksel	63
9. Zara	75
10. Aksel	83
11. Zara	93
12. Aksel	101
13. Zara	115
14. Aksel	123
15. Zara	129
16. Zara	139
17. Aksel	145
18. Zara	155
19. Zara	159
20. Aksel	165
21. Zara	171
22. Aksel	177
23. Zara	187
24. Aksel	193
25. Zara	205

26. Aksel	211
27. Epilogue	219
About the Author	229
Also by this author	231

DEDICATION

To all the girls who wouldn't mind being chased through the woods by a masked hunter and made to scream all night long...

PLAYLIST

Hunted playlist

"RAVE"—Dxrk ダーク
"The wolf in your darkest room"—Matthew Mayfield
"To my knees"—Two feet
"If I didn't know better"—Mack Lorén
"Shut up and listen"—Nicholas Bonnin, Angelicca
"HEARTBEAT"—Isabel LaRosa
"Make me feel"—Elvis Drew
"I'm yours"—Isabel LaRosa
"Miss YOU!"—Corpse
"MIDDLE OF THE NIGHT"—Ellen Duhé
"KILL ANYONE"—Two Feet ft. Ali Abdul
"I did something bad"—Taylor Swift
"Waiting Game"—BANKS
"Crazy in love"—Sofia Karlberg

You can find the playlist on Spotify here

AUTHOR'S NOTE

This story explores dark romance and contains explicit content that may not be suitable for all readers. It includes themes of dominance, psychotic behavior, possessiveness, and explicit mature scenes presented alongside delicate subject matters that may be distressing or triggering for some individuals.

Please refer to the comprehensive list of warnings on my website for detailed information on potential triggers.

I advise reader discretion and recommend only proceeding if you're comfortable with the mentioned themes. Rest assured, the story ends in a HEA with no cliffhanger or cheating between the main characters.

1

ZARA

The plane shudders violently as we hit another pocket of turbulence. I grip the armrests until my knuckles turn white, peering out the window. Sheets of rain distort the Norwegian landscape into a colorless blur far below.

This is exactly the extreme weather I had hoped to study when my boss sent me on this research trip to northern Scandinavia. But staring it down on the other side of a screen from the safety of my Minneapolis office and being tossed around by the merciless skies are vastly different experiences.

"Try not to worry. We'll be on the ground shortly."

The deep, lightly accented voice comes from the man beside me. I turn to find piercing eyes studying me with faint amusement. In the tight confines of our economy seats, I can't help but notice how solidly built he is—like he was chiseled from granite.

"I'm not worried," I lie, color rising to my cheeks at

being so easily read. "A little turbulence doesn't bother me."

One side of his mouth quirks upwards in a knowing smirk. "You don't need to be stoic. My name is Tor. Please allow me to welcome you to Norway properly." The large, calloused hand he offers completely engulfs my own as we shake.

"Zara," I reply, trying not to stare too openly. He has sharp features and a predatory look to him.

"So what brings a beautiful woman like yourself to Norway, Zara?"

Beautiful? I blink, caught off guard by the bold compliment. "I'm an atmospheric scientist. Here to study the weather patterns."

Tor's smirk deepens into a full grin, revealing crooked white teeth. "You've come to the right place for extreme conditions."

As if to prove his point, the plane gives another sickening lurch. I grab my laptop bag and passport from under the seat, clinging to them tightly. Something to cling to as an all-consuming fear that we're going to crash and die hits me.

"Try to relax and enjoy the ride," Tor says. His eyes flash as if he finds my discomfort amusing. "Where you're headed, you'll no doubt have more turbulent conditions than this."

"The difference is my feet will be firmly on the ground," I respond.

Forcing myself to calm down, I glance out the window into the clouds. My pre-arranged host, Aksel, should be waiting for me at the airport when I land. My boss somehow found his contact details through an online ad since the area where he wants me to study the weather patterns is sparsely populated, and we exchanged a few emails. He's a solitary man living alone in the wilderness who has agreed to put me up and be my guide for my research.

But as the plane rocks and shutters through another vicious burst of turbulence, I can't help but feel a stab of trepidation.

What exactly have I gotten myself into by venturing into the storm-tossed heart of Norway?

The plane finally smacks down violently on the rain-slicked runway in Tromsø. As the cabin fills with the whir of the flaps being extended, I blow out a long, relieved breath. We've made it through the terrible storm in one piece.

Tor retrieves his bag from the overhead bin like we hadn't just been tossed around for the last hour. "This is where I take my leave, Zara. Safe travels, and try to enjoy the solitude." He winks one of those piercing eyes and then disappears down the aisle without another word.

I have to wait until I'm one of the last to deplane. As I duck through the hatch, a cold blast of wind and driving rain smacks me fully in the face; so much for my carefully styled hair and makeup. I hunch my shoulders against the deluge, quickly retreating into the heated and warm terminal, thankful when I'm out of the stormy weather.

I breeze through passport control, grab a luggage cart, and wait for my equipment to arrive at the carousel. When it finally arrives, I struggle to load it onto the trolley and then push it toward the exit.

Aksel agreed he'd be waiting outside the terminal, so I pushed the car outside and ducked under the awning to wait for my ride.

I see him holding up a card with my name on it—a lone, towering figure standing apart from the crowd. Even from half a dozen yards, I can make out the chiseled angles of his face, dark hair dripping from the downpour. He doesn't bother trying to stay dry, taking the onslaught of rain with a stoic indifference.

Our eyes meet as I approach. His gaze, nearly as dark as the storm clouds massing overhead, roams too deliberately over the lines of my body. I instantly regret wearing my fitted blouse and slacks—they're completely inadequate for this harsh climate.

"You must be Zara Driscoll," the man states when I'm within earshot, making no effort to raise his voice over the gale. His lightly accented English still manages to carry weight and timbre.

Up close, I can see that he is powerfully built and over six feet four inches tall. Rain plasters his snug charcoal sweater to the contours of his chest and arms, and runic black ink trails along thick forearms and up his biceps. Dark stubble ghosts his chiseled jawline, complementing his handsome looks.

I offer my hand. "Yes, you must be Aksel. It's a pleasure to meet you."

Aksel regards my outreached hand for a pause before

finally taking it briefly in a calloused grip. I do my best not to shiver at his touch.

"We should go. The storm is getting worse." He turns abruptly and strides off without checking if I'm following.

I push the cart at almost a jog to keep up with his long-legged gait. We reach a mud-splattered jeep where Aksel stows my bags and equipment in the back. I hurry to the passenger side, anxious to escape the rain, only to find the door won't open.

A loud crunch of footsteps comes up behind me before a large hand shoves the door open. Aksel's hulking form looms so close that his chest nearly presses against my back. I flush at the sudden proximity, unnerved by his disregard for personal space.

His voice is low and dark beside my ear as he leans in. "You'll find things are a bit different rustic out here, Miss Driscoll."

I swallow hard, chilled not by the rain but by the man I'm due to stay with. A tremor of unease goes through me at the unmistakable darkness in his tone.

What have I gotten myself into by coming here alone to study storms at the edge of nowhere?

In that moment, I realize my greatest danger may not be the storms and blistering winds of this stark, unforgiving land. It may be the brooding, potentially unhinged man I've hired to keep me alive.

We drive in tense silence for what feels like an eternity. The jeep's windshield wipers can barely keep up with the torrential downpour pounding the glass. I clutch the door handle until my knuckles turn white, stealing sidelong glances at my host.

Aksel doesn't speak a word or even spare me a look. His chiseled profile is rigidly set, biceps flexing as he wrestles with the steering wheel against the punishing gales. His dark eyes stare unblinkingly through the rain-streaked windshield. I can't shake the feeling that he's resenting having to play chauffeur or simply resenting my presence here.

The nameless dread that seized me back at the airport steadily grows with every mile the jeep eats across the sodden landscape. We head deeper and deeper into the uninhabited wilderness, putting more distance between myself and any semblance of civilization.

Finally, after what has to be at least an hour, if not more, Aksel kills the engine. I blink in confusion, peering through the pounding deluge. All I can see is the looming shape of fir trees massed around a small clearing. And there, nestled amongst the dripping pines, is a rustic cabin with smoke coiling upwards from the chimney.

Is this where he lives? My research bunker for the next month?

Aksel doesn't wait for me. In a flash, he's out of the jeep and headed for the cabin, rain instantly flattening his thick dark hair against his skull. I scramble to follow, the downpour soaking me to the bone by the time we're stomping up the creaky porch steps.

My host pauses long enough to throw me a look over his shoulder. Those eyes undress me with their stare, burning my shivering skin beneath the drenched clothes.

Then he wrenches open the cabin door and ducks inside without a word.

I practically tumble in after Aksel, gripping the wall until my vision adjusts to the dimly lit interior. The air is warm with the piney scent of a smoldering fire in the massive stone hearth. Candles and lanterns glow softly over a modest but comfortable living area with overstuffed chairs and animal skin rugs.

It's all delightfully rustic, the perfect setting for getting in touch with Mother Nature's raw power. Condensation from my damp clothes begins fogging the windowpanes, overlooking the driving rain and skeletal trees bending against the tempest outside.

The cabin door creaks closed behind me, making me jump. I spin to find Aksel behind me, lips set in a grim line beneath those striking cheekbones and gray eyes. His heavy wool sweater clings in all the right places, outlining the rugged contours of his muscular frame. With his height, the effect is innately intimidating and arousing.

"This will be your home for the duration of your research," he states flatly.

My unease grows at his choice of words. My home? I'm a professional here for work, not to make myself at home with this strange, uncommunicative loner.

An icy shiver skates down my spine that has nothing to do with my wet clothes. Aksel stares at me with an unsettling intensity, like a coiled predator waiting to pounce.

I get the distinct impression that I may be the prey.

2

AKSEL

The blonde shakes out her drenched hair, glancing around my cabin. Her full lips are parted, those green eyes wide with what? Fear? Excitement? Uncertainty?

I can't quite read the emotion flickering within, but it doesn't matter. The second Zara Driscoll stepped across my threshold, she ceased being a person. She became a thing—an object for me to possess and defile.

My cock is achingly hard just from the sight of her in those soaked clothes. The flimsy fabric clings so tantalizingly to the curves of her tits and the flare of her hips that it's obscene. I have an overwhelming urge to rip those garments from her and fuck her against the wall.

Claim her fully as my own so she can never escape me.

I shouldn't feel this way—not after weeks of meticulous planning and preparation to hunt her like the helpless prey she is. But something about Zara stokes the raging bonfire of my desires into an inferno.

During the drive, I carefully schooled my expression and body language into that of a cold, indifferent host, trying to seduce her into a false sense of security so she would be too distracted by my manner to detect the steel trap closing around her.

Yet weeks of calculated planning come undone with her standing in my home, droplets from her sopping hair rolling down the soft, pale skin of her neck and disappearing beneath the neckline of her blouse. The hunter's restraint and patience are shredded by a primal, untamed need to claim her in an utterly different way.

The silence between us is deafening—the void filled only by the crackle of the fire in the hearth and the wail of the storm raging outside. I can feel her uncertainty like a living force between us.

I take a deliberate step forward, closing the distance until I inhale her crisp, clean fragrance. Zara instinctively retreats a step, her back hitting the wall. Her eyes lock onto mine, reflecting confusion and a flicker of dismay as I prowl ever nearer.

"You need to get out of those wet clothes before you catch a chill," I murmur, deliberately allowing my eyes to travel down the lines of her body as if I'm visualizing peeling each soaked layer from her.

She crosses her arms over her chest, swallowing hard. "I...I don't have anything dry to change into," Zara stammers. "My luggage is still out in the jeep."

"I've got clothes you can borrow." I take another calculated step forward until my body almost grazes hers. Her scent is a siren's call, luring me to run my hands over every sweet curve and soft hollow of her flesh until I know her form as intimately as I know my own.

She shrinks back against the wall. Her eyes have widened into saucers, and her pupils dilate with what has to be fear.

Good. I want her scared of me.

"A-alright," she concedes, unable to disguise the tremor in her voice. "If you could just get me a change of clothes…"

My mouth curves into a smile. "I'll take you to my room and find something to slip into. This way."

I gesture for her to follow, then turn on my heel and stride through the living area. A glimpse over my shoulder confirms she is rooted in place, clearly considering disobeying my suggestion. Foolish girl.

"Did you mishear me, Miss Driscoll? I said this way to my room." My tone dips into a low, gravelly command.

The way her teeth dig into her plump lower lip tells me she is seriously debating how to handle the situation. But the predator in me finds her feigned bravery and insubordination irresistibly intoxicating. Such innocence and resistance only inflame my need to break her to my will. I continue to my room, grab a pair of jogging pants and a flannel shirt, and place them on the bed. Once I turn around, she's still nowhere to be seen.

I leave and find her lingering in the hallway, looking like a frightened rabbit caught in headlights. "You can change in there." I nod toward the bedroom.

Zara brushes past me warily. The scent of vanilla and roses infiltrates my senses like a narcotic. My lips part instinctively to draw in a lungful of her intoxicating aroma —vanilla and rain-soaked roses with an underlying musk that has my mouth watering.

It takes every ounce of self-discipline not to grab a fistful of her golden hair and drag her against me. To pin that lithe body flush against mine so she could feel the undeniable evidence of my need for her. So she knows there's nowhere she can run—no escape.

Zara disappears into my bedroom, shutting the door firmly in my face. I can hear the telltale sounds of her shimmying out of those form-fitting wet clothes: the rustle of damp fabric sliding over damp skin, the whisper of a zipper being pulled down.

The mental picture has my cock straining shamelessly against the prison of my jeans. I give in to temptation and palm the aching length, biting back a guttural groan. If the thought of her undressing is this maddening, how far will I be pushed once she's finally laid bare before me?

A harsh rasp comes from the other side of the door. "Aksel...?"

Her timid call rakes its nails down the length of my fraying restraint. I take my hand off my cock before responding gruffly, "Yes?"

"Where...um, where exactly did you leave the clothes for me?"

The naked vulnerability in her voice is like a physical caress against my cock. I can imagine those full, pink lips parting while I shoved it into her throat. My jaw ticks as I grind my molars, fighting back the basest of instincts. How easy it would be to barge through that door and end this game right now on my terms.

"They're on the bed," I reply roughly. "A flannel shirt and some sweatpants that'll be too large but better than nothing."

"Oh...okay, thanks."

Silence falls, the loudest sounds being the ragged rasp of my breathing and the thrumming of my pulse between my ears. I pivot to lean my forehead against the smooth wooden door. When my eyes fall closed, I can almost envision her on the other side—droplets clinging to the slopes of her bare breasts, trailing icy paths down the flat plane of her stomach to where her tight little cunt waits.

Enough!

I give a violent shake of my head and straighten, running both hands through my damp hair. I need to put some space between myself and the temptation on the other side of this door before I lose control. Before the predator inside me descends on the girl who is changing just feet away.

"I'll make some coffee," I toss over my shoulder, already walking from the hallway before she can reply. "Take your time."

I practically flee into the living room and beeline for the small kitchen, desperate to put physical and mental distance between myself and Zara. My muscles are rigid with the strain of controlling my baser urges. My breaths come in sharp pants, nostrils flaring like a bull's as I work to bring my raging hormones back under control.

Seizing the coffee grounds, I yank open the cabinet and fumble for a filter with shaking hands. I need a distraction, a tether to hold me steady before I spiral into the depths of my depravity.

Because if I thought my fantasies of hunting Zara Driscoll were dark before, they're nothing compared to what's percolated in the twisted recesses of my psyche since laying eyes on her in person.

My sordid imagination feasts on the ripe reality of her pliant body, shuddering at each gasped plea as I shatter her and take everything she has to give. To hear her cry and beg and scream as I unleash the full ferocity of my desires on her.

The images have me squeezing the counter's edge in a white-knuckled grip. My cock is a steel rod grinding against the zipper of my jeans with each slight shift.

How am I supposed to look into those clear green eyes again as she obliviously puts her life into my calloused hands? When all I want is to ruin her—to destroy her in both body and spirit?

Morality has never been an issue; after all, I intended to hunt her like an animal. Kill her. And yet, this seems so much worse because what I want to do to her means it's never over. She'll be mine forever.

Zara has awakened a long-dormant devil inside me that I fear may be too powerful to contain.

Is bringing her here to my isolated lair a terrible, unforgivable mistake that will end in tragedy?

But as her soft footfalls sound behind me, I turn with a carefully veiled expression to find her swimming in my oversized shirt. And there's no denying the truth in the pit of my stomach:

It's already too late to turn back.

3

ZARA

The hot mug of coffee warms my chilled hands. I steal glances at Aksel across the rustic kitchen table. He hasn't said a word since grunting for me to take a seat when I shuffled back into the living area in his oversized shirt and joggers, which are swimming off my hips. He sits hunched over his steaming mug, alternating between staring broodingly into the inky liquid and shooting me brief looks that set my nerves jangling.

Aksel's body is slightly angled away from me. Still, I can't help noticing the taut lines of his shoulders outlining the contours of hard, knotted muscle beneath his snug thermal shirt. In the flickering glow from the fireplace, I can make out the stark, sinewy cords of his forearms disappearing beneath the shoved-up sleeves. Every part of him seems densely packed with power scarcely leashed beneath his granite exterior.

I have to resist the urge to squirm in my chair as my gaze involuntarily drops to the prominent bulge tenting his lap. Even when sitting, there's no disguising the distinctly male endowment evident in Aksel's loose sweatpants he changed into after I left his room. Heat steals across my cheeks and chest when I realize I'm staring.

Years of solitude in the isolated wilderness likely breeds a certain lack of inhibition. Aksel probably doesn't even realize how easily I can make out the thick outline and shape of his—

"Is the coffee to your satisfaction, or were you hoping for something else to warm you up?"

Aksel's low, gravelly voice jerks me out of my thoughts. I look up, flustered, to find those glacial blue eyes drilling into me with dark intensity. My breath catches at the implication in his words and that I got caught staring at this guy's cock.

"N-no, the coffee is fine, thanks." I hastily drop my gaze down to my mug again, stirring the dark liquid with a spoon, having no other excuse to avoid his smoldering stare. "It's, um, it's been a long journey, so this really hits the spot."

For a stretch, the only sounds are the crackle of fire in the hearth and the insistent drumming of rain against the cabin windows. Then Aksel makes a low rumbling noise in his throat—between a dry chuckle and a grunt of sardonic acknowledgment. "And your journey has only just begun."

My cheeks burn hotter. Slowly, I risk lifting my gaze again to find my host openly regarding me. The way his eyes leisurely trail over every line and curve of my body makes me shudder—whether from discomfort or something more illicit, I can't tell.

Aksel doesn't try to mask his perusal like most men would. Instead, there's a confrontational quality to how he looks at me. In the heavy silence, it's as if he's staking an indisputable claim to having free rein over every inch of me.

My eyes reflexively drop once more to the unmistakable erection straining against his sweatpants. This time, his lips twist into a ghost of a knowing smirk before taking a slow, deliberate swig of coffee.

"It's been a long time since I've had a guest," he murmurs into his mug. "This cabin can get quite cold and lonely without company."

The statement causes my heart to lodge in my throat. My hands grip my mug tighter, and every nerve prickles with an unsettling awareness of being utterly alone with Aksel deep in this wilderness sanctuary of his. Isolated and cut off from the outside world, I am at his mercy entirely.

"Well, I certainly hope I won't be imposing too much," I reply, proud of how steady I keep my voice. "Once the weather clears, I'll need to head out to the areas mapped for data collection as soon as possible."

Aksel sets his mug down, eyeing me over the rim with a look that could cut glass. "This is my territory, Miss Driscoll. My rules. You'll go nowhere without my guidance and approval—and certainly not until the storms have passed completely." His nostrils flare as he holds my gaze in a silent battle of wills. "Is that understood?"

I give a jerky nod, unable to find my voice under the weight of that stare.

Rising from his seat, he circles around behind me. I feel

rather than see his looming presence at my back as he leans close, braced against the table. The clean, earthy scent of him crashes over me in an overwhelming wave.

"This isn't a civilized place that follows society's rules, Miss Driscoll," Aksel rumbles, sending a shiver cracking down my spine. His heated breath brushes the sensitive skin at the back of my neck, raising goosebumps in its wake. "Out here in the harsh, uncivilized lands, only one rule matters—the strongest will survive."

Every muscle in my body has gone rigid. It's as if I can sense the predator baring its fangs and readying its jaws to devour me.

Aksel leans closer still. Thick, inescapable tension saturates the air. My heart thunders so violently in my ears that I almost miss the velvet growl of his next words:

"And I'm the apex predator here."

I can't stop the shudder that ripples through me. Every instinct screams at me to get up and flee, to put as much distance between myself and this man as possible. But some deeper, more primal part of me seems to have gone utterly still and calm in the face of his blatant threat.

I watch the bulging cords of muscle in Aksel's powerful forearms flex and shift as he braces his weight on the table, caging me in while he remains behind me. I can't tear my gaze away from the ink on his arms.

"You'll remain here until I deem it safe to proceed with your research. And you'll do exactly as I say without question or hesitation."

His head dips lower, the stubbled line of his jaw grazing the side of my neck. I can't stifle the whimper that escapes when his lips brush against the shell of my ear. "Do you understand, Miss Driscoll?" The proximity to such a powerful man sends a jolt to my core. Each consonant is precisely enunciated, underscored by his teeth grazing against my skin.

I give a tremulous nod, my throat too constricted to speak. Aksel's satisfied rumble of approval vibrates against me.

"Good girl." The timbre of his praise reverberates straight to my core, making me clench my thighs together. "I enjoy it when my guests learn to follow the rules."

He straightens and steps away slowly, allowing me to draw a shuddering breath as the charged tension abruptly dissipates. I almost mourn the loss of his presence surrounding me until I risk a glance up at him.

Aksel is eyeing me with a look of dark, ravenous hunger, and his cock is tenting his sweatpants. A sly, knowing smirk curves his lips when our gazes lock, and he makes no effort to conceal his arousal. Not that he could. It's huge and impossible to ignore.

"We'll have such fun together, Miss Driscoll." His tongue darts out to wet his lips. "So very much fun..."

Accepting this trip might have been a mistake.

4

AKSEL

The rain pelts down on the rusty tin roof of the carport, a steady thrum that drowns out all other sounds. I slide out from under my truck, wiping the grease from my hands onto a stained rag. My muscles ache from the physical labor, but it is a welcome distraction from the temptation sleeping just inside.

Zara.

The mere name sends a shiver down my spine. I can picture her now, tangled in the sheets, that golden hair spilling across the pillow. How easily I could slip into the bedroom, pin her delicate wrists above her head as she gasped in surprise...

I shake my head, gritting my teeth and forcing the thought away. Grabbing a wrench, I slide back under the truck's chassis, letting the rhythmic clanging of metal on metal overwhelm my senses.

It has been so long since I've had a woman in my territory. The rush of power and the thrill of subjugation are intoxicating. Zara's innocence is like a magnet to me, an untapped well of passion waiting to be broken open.

The wrench slips in my grip, clattering to the concrete. I curse under my breath and roll out to retrieve it. Through the curtain of rain, I catch a glimpse of movement from the cabin window.

Zara. Awake at last.

My body tenses, coiled like a snake about to strike. I can almost taste the metallic tang of her fear on my tongue. One misstep and those big green eyes would widen in terror as I showed her how merciless the wilderness could be.

The soft pitter-patter of footsteps on the porch makes me freeze. Zara emerges, wrapped in a blanket against the chill. Her gaze sweeps across the yard before settling on me, half-hidden under the truck.

Our eyes meet, and I see it there—a flicker of fear. It's good. She is starting to understand how isolated we are and how there is no escape from me.

A smile tugs at the corners of my mouth as I rise to my feet, the rain plastering my shirt to the contours of my chest.

She's watching me.

The thought sends a thrill down my spine as I straighten up from beneath the truck, rain sluicing down my face and chest. Zara's wide eyes find mine from across the yard.

I allow my gaze to rake over her, taking in the delicate curves outlined beneath that thin blanket. Her fingers clutch the fabric tighter as I stalk toward her, water squelching beneath my boots.

"Did you sleep well?" I ask. Up close, I detect her pulse fluttering rapidly in the hollow of her throat. Her lips part as if to answer, but she doesn't speak.

Reaching out, I hook a finger under the edge of the blanket and tug it down, exposing the shirt she's wearing. Zara gasps, a blossom of color rising in her cheeks, but she doesn't pull away.

"You're soaked," she murmurs, her gaze dropping to my shirt plastered against my chest. "You'll catch your death out here."

A chuckle spills from my lips as I close the distance between us. She shrinks back against the cabin wall, blanket clutched to her chest like a shield. I lean in close enough for our bodies to share warmth, letting my eyes bore into hers.

"I'm not so easy to kill, little bird." My fingers find her jaw, tilting her face up to mine. "Don't worry about me. I'm the one you should be afraid of…"

She glares up at me, those emerald eyes flashing with defiance. "Why exactly?"

My lips curl at her bravado. So she wants to play brave, does she? I'll soon rid her of that naivete.

Sliding my hand from her jaw, I trail my fingertips down the slender column of her neck. Zara stiffens but doesn't pull away as I trace the throbbing pulse point beneath her ear.

"You're out here all alone with me. No one for miles to hear you scream." I lean in until my lips graze the shell of her ear, letting my hot breath fan across her skin. "I could do anything I want to you, and no one would stop me."

A tremor runs through her, and I revel in how her pupils blow wide with fear. Still, she holds my stare, that stubborn jaw setting in determination.

"You won't, though." It's a question as much as a statement, wavering ever so slightly.

Holding her gaze captive, I grip her chin between my thumb and forefinger. "And what makes you so sure about that?"

For a beat, she's silent, carefully weighing her next words. "If you wanted to hurt me, you would have done it already." Her voice is soft. "You had plenty of chances on that drive here or last night."

"Who said anything about hurting you?" I move my hand from her chin to the back of her neck. "There are other ways I can make you scream."

I relish the flush of color that creeps into her cheeks, the telltale widening of her pupils. She is turned on, whether she'll admit it or not. The thought sends a spike of arousal through me, but I force it down.

Clearing my throat, I take a small step back, giving her some space. "You must be hungry. Can I fix you some breakfast?"

Zara blinks, looking momentarily confused by the abrupt change in topic. "Oh, um, sure. That would be great, thanks."

"Good. You go on inside and get warmed up. I'll be in shortly."

She nods, clutching the blanket tighter around her slim

shoulders as she turns toward the cabin. I watch her retreat, admiring the sway of her hips.

Ducking back under the carport, I grab a rag and wipe the grease from my hands and arms. The physical labor has done little to distract me from her temptation. But I must be patient because rushing things now wouldn't be wise. All my plans shattered last night, and I need to reevaluate my next steps.

Once I'm sufficiently cleaned up, I head into the house. Zara sits at the small kitchen table, blanket draped around her. She offers me a tentative smile as I enter.

"I hope you're in the mood for eggs," I say, moving toward the stove. "It's about all I've got at the moment."

"Eggs sound great."

I can feel her eyes on me as I work, cracking the eggs into a bowl and whisking them together. The domesticity of the scene feels strange. I'm used to being alone and having Zara in my space makes everything feel off-kilter.

When the eggs are cooked, I serve them on two plates with toast. Zara thanks me when I set the plate down in front of her.

"Eat up," I say, sitting across from her. "You'll need your strength to survive this place."

She nods, picking up her fork. I watch her over my own plate, hyper-aware of every small movement. She tucks her hair behind her ear, the flutter of her lashes as she glances at me and then away. So innocent. So ripe for the taking.

I spear another bite of eggs, tearing my gaze away. I had intended to lure her out into the wilderness and take my time hunting and playing with her before putting a quick end to it. A hunting accident, a tragic disappearance—the wilderness has a way of swallowing up the weak. No one would've batted an eye at a scientist going missing here. It's the way I keep my hunger for blood under control, luring unsuspecting tourists here under the pretext of help.

But one look into those wide, innocent eyes and my plans unraveled like a stray thread pulled loose. The temptation to claim her, to strip away that naive purity and make her truly mine, is overwhelming. Like a wolf scenting its mate, my most primal instincts were instantly, irrevocably triggered.

I squeeze my eyes shut, pinching the bridge of my nose.

Fuck's sake Aksel, get a grip before you do something rash and ruin everything.

Taking slow, even breaths, I force myself to focus on the sound of the rain pattering against the roof.

In through the nose, out through the mouth. Steady and calm.

When I open my eyes again, Zara watches me with that same cautious curiosity as if sensing the war raging inside me. A shiver rolls down my spine, and I grip the table's edge to avoid reaching for her and pulling her into my lap.

"Is everything okay?" she asks.

I nod once, fixing her with an inscrutable stare. "Just need some air."

Rising abruptly from the table, I make my way toward the door. Zara doesn't try to stop me as I pull on my boots and jacket, letting the door slam shut behind me.

When I step onto the porch, the crisp scent of pine and

fresh rain hits me. I inhale deeply, letting it clear my head. Out here, surrounded by the looming trees and rugged peaks, I can almost convince myself I'm still in control.

Almost.

Jaw clenched tight, I start pacing the porch like a caged animal. The wet boards slap against the soles of my boots, the rhythmic sound helping to soothe the savage creature pacing inside me.

I am the master of my own fate. I've spent years cultivating my skills, honing myself into the perfect apex predator. Stalking, subduing, killing—it's what I was born for. And no pretty little thing will derail me, no matter how intoxicating she might be.

Slowing to a stop at the far end of the porch, I brace my hands on the damp railing and gaze out over the forest. The heavy clouds have parted just enough to allow a few slanting rays of sunlight to streak through, gilding the rain-soaked trees and peaks in soft golden light.

I take another deep, steadying breath and nod once to myself.

Time to get back on track.

5

ZARA

It's as if I've woken up in either a dark romance story or a fucking horror story, and I'm not sure which yet. I watch my host as he prowls back and forth on the porch. His eyes are intense and unfocused like he's battling some inner demon that I can't begin to understand.

Part of me longs to escape, to put as much distance as possible between myself and this isolated cabin and its unhinged owner. But the scientist in me knows that fleeing into the storm would be suicide. I'm trapped here, at least until the weather clears up a bit. The very thought makes my chest tighten with fear.

Aksel stops pacing and turns his piercing gaze toward the window, catching me watching him. I freeze, feeling like a mouse watched by a hungry cat. His full lips curl into a wicked smile, revealing straight white teeth. He knows I'm afraid of him. And I think he likes it.

With a few long strides, he crosses the porch and

throws the cabin door open, the icy rain gusting behind him. "See something you like?" he rumbles, his voice as deep and rough as grinding boulders.

I try to keep my voice from shaking. "I was just wondering what you were doing out there," I say.

"Getting some air." He runs a hand through his dark hair, slicking it back from his chiseled face. "Didn't mean to make you nervous."

The way his eyes rake over my body tells me he's lying through his teeth. I tug self-consciously at the oversized shirt he gave me, struggling not to squirm under his intense stare.

"You're safe here with me," he says, crossing the room until he's looming over me. "As long as you do exactly what I say."

I nod, my throat too tight with fear to speak. Aksel's eyes bore into mine, daring me to disobey. His proximity is overwhelming—I can smell sweat, motor oil, and some deep, musky scent that must be purely him. It makes my head swim.

"Good girl," he rumbles, brushing a damp strand of hair from my face. His calloused fingers trail along my jawline, and I can't suppress a shudder. "We're going to get along just fine here, you and I."

I want to ask him what he means by that, but I'm still trying to figure out the answer. Aksel seems to sense my unease, and his full lips twist into that predatory smile again.

"Why don't you go get cleaned up and dressed into your own clothes?" he suggests, nodding toward my case he must have retrieved from the Jeep this morning. "I'll get the fire going again. Wouldn't want you catching a chill."

It's not really a suggestion, and we both know it. Still, I'm grateful for the chance to escape from under his scorching gaze. I grab my case and hurry into the bathroom, closing the door and leaning against it with a shuddering exhale.

Get a grip, Zara, I tell myself sternly. He's just a little intense, that's all. You're a grown woman and a respected scientist. Don't let some weird, super-hot Norwegian guy intimidate you.

But even as I try to bolster my courage, I can't shake the feeling that I'm prey. Aksel moves with a dangerous, almost feral grace. And those eyes—I've never seen a man look at me with such blatant possession before.

I take a deep, shuddering breath as I look at my reflection in the steamy mirror. My cheeks are flushed, my green eyes wide with fear and desire? No, that can't be it—not for a man like Aksel.

But even as I try to push the thought away, my gaze is drawn to his oversized shirt. It hangs off one shoulder, the worn fabric soft against my skin. I can't help wondering what it would be like to have his strong hands on me instead of the cotton.

Stop it, I scold myself firmly. He's not just intense. He's dangerous. The way he looks at me like he wants to devour me whole. A shiver runs down my spine, not entirely from fear this time.

This is absurd. I'm a trainee scientist. I've never let a

man rattle me before. Hell, I'm a virgin, for God's sake. But then, I've also never met a man like Aksel.

The sheer size of him is enough to make my knees go weak. He has to be at least six foot four with a powerful, muscular frame covered in ink. And those eyes—a gray-blue that bores holes straight through me.

When he touched me, trailing those rough fingertips along my skin, I felt like lightning struck me. The memory of it makes me shiver, my nipples tightening beneath the thin fabric of his shirt.

What is wrong with me? This man is clearly unhinged, probably a psychopath. I should be terrified, not aroused. But I can't seem to help myself.

He moves with a predatory grace, like a great jungle cat studying its prey. And I have the sinking feeling that I'm the prey being stalked. The thought should frighten me. It does, in a way—that tight, anxious knot in my stomach that screams at me to run. But there's another part of me, a darker part, that wants to see what he's capable of.

What would it be like to be possessed by a man like that? To have all that raw power and intensity focused solely on me? A tremor runs through me at the thought, my thighs clenching instinctively.

Outside the bathroom door, I hear the fire crackle and the rain hissing against the roof and windows. Any sane person would be trying to formulate an escape plan right now, considering how he's acted. We're trapped in here with nothing to do. But all I can think about is the dangerous, beautiful beast waiting for me on the other side of that door.

6

AKSEL

After what feels like an age, Zara returns to the living room, and my jaw falls to the floor.

That dress shatters any resolve I had left. My mouth goes dry, drinking in her curves, the fabric clinging to her body in a way that makes my blood heat. Her blonde hair cascades over her shoulders, and I ache to run my fingers through those silky strands.

I take a shuddering breath as Zara settles onto the couch, trying and failing to keep my eyes off her body. The dress hugs her curves, the neckline plunging dangerously low. She crosses her legs demurely, utterly oblivious to the effect she's having on me.

"You look stunning," I force out, my voice a guttural growl. Never before has Aksel fucking Nilsen given a woman a compliment before, yet here we are.

Zara blushes, a rosy hue spreading across those high cheekbones. "Thank you," she murmurs, ducking her head shyly.

The motion draws my gaze to her tits straining against the fabric, and I dig my nails into my palms to keep from reaching out and ripping that flimsy material right off her body.

She clears her throat. "Sorry, is it too much? I can change into something more appropriate." Zara moves to stand.

"No!" The word bursts from me before I can stop it, far too forceful. Zara freezes, eyes wide with surprise and a flicker of fear. I take a calming breath through my nose. "You look perfect just as you are."

Her tongue darts out to wet those plump lips, and I track the movement hungrily. So innocent, so tempting. She settles back against the cushions, squirming under my scrutiny.

"Would you like a drink?" I offer, needing something to distract me before I pounce on her.

Zara nods, worrying her full bottom lip between her teeth. The sight of that lush mouth being abused sends a jolt straight to my cock. I grip the arm of the chair, knuckles whitening as I try to get a grip.

Moving to the small bar, I pour two glasses of the expensive scotch I keep on hand, letting the familiar ritual calm me. When I turn back with the tumblers, Zara has one knee drawn up, skimming that tantalizing hemline even higher. My steps falter, and it's a fucking fight not to drop to my knees and bury my face between those thighs.

For weeks, I'd planned her demise, intending to lure her out into the forest before stalking and then striking. A clean kill, then I could dispose of the body without a trace. But now... now those plans seem laughable.

Zara wasn't sent here to die. She was delivered to me, a gift from the gods to sate my darkest desires.

I don't know how long I can deny my body's cravings while I drink in every luscious curve, every tantalizing glimpse of skin. My mouth waters at the thought of tasting her. But for so long, I've avoided such proclivities for a reason. I can't turn into my father.

Our fingers brush when I hand her the drink, and electricity crackles between us. She sucks in a sharp breath, pupils widening.

"Thank you," Zara whispers, her voice a breathless caress that has me clenching my fists to keep from grabbing her.

I give a tight nod, sinking into the chair across from her. From this angle, I can see straight down the tempting V of her neckline. It would be so easy to rip that fabric aside and bury my face between her tits.

Downing my scotch in one burning swallow, I set the glass aside with a trembling hand.

A predatory grin stretches my lips as I lean forward, bracing my elbows on my knees.

Zara's chest rises and falls rapidly with each panted exhale. She clears her throat. "Would you like me to make us lunch?" she asks.

The innocent question snaps me back to reality, the sound of her sweet voice cutting through the haze of lust fogging my brain. I blink slowly, tamping down the raging beast within me that demands I take her right here on this very couch.

"Lunch?" I rasp.

She nods, worrying her plump bottom lip between her teeth. The motion draws my gaze inexorably to her mouth, and I imagine those lips stretched obscenely wide around my cock.

I grind my teeth. "Yes, that would be nice."

A relieved smile curves those tempting lips, and she rises gracefully from the couch. The dress rides up as she stands, giving me a teasing glimpse of the edge of her black lacy panties, making my mouth water.

"I can whip up a quiche if you have the ingredients?" Zara offers, tucking a stray lock of blonde hair behind her ear.

I grunt an affirmative, trying and failing to tear my eyes away from her tits, straining against the fabric with each breath. "There should be eggs and vegetables in the fridge. Flour in the cupboard, too, I think."

"Perfect!" She beams at me, all sunshine and innocence.

I can only nod, mesmerized by the sway of her hips as she turns and heads for the small kitchen. From this angle, I get a perfect view of the gentle flare of her hips into the lush curves of her ass barely contained by that sinful dress.

Sinking back against the couch, I palm the aching bulge in my pants and grit my teeth against a groan. Zara bends over to retrieve something from the fridge, that dress riding up to reveal a better glimpse of her panties.

Fucking hell, I'm going to ravage her before this day is through.

My cock throbs at the thought, straining against the denim in a way that's damn near painful. I rub my length through the rough fabric, reveling in the delicious friction.

The soft sounds of Zara puttering around in the kitchen only stoke the flames higher. My eyes slip shut as I imagine her on her knees before me, those pretty lips stretched wide as she takes me right into the back of her throat.

"So, Aksel," she says conversationally as she cracks eggs into a bowl. "What do you do for a living out here?"

I force my eyes open. "I'm a hunter," I grunt.

Those big green eyes meet mine as she stands at the counter facing me. "Really? That must be fascinating work."

A harsh laugh escapes me before I can bite it back. "If you say so."

She frowns at my tone but doesn't question it, simply returning her attention to whisking the eggs.

"And you?" I ask gruffly. "What brings a pretty thing like you to the middle of nowhere? You never said what research you're conducting in our correspondence."

A delicate flush stains her cheeks when I call her pretty. "I'm an atmospheric scientist," she explains. "I'm here to study weather patterns in the area."

My brow furrows, trying to picture this sweet, soft creature braving the harsh wilderness to get weather readings. The thought makes something dark and protective unfurl in my chest. "Seems like dangerous work."

She smiles as she chops vegetables. "I may be small, but I'm stronger than I look."

My eyes narrow as I drink in the flex of lean muscle in her arms, the determined set of her jaw. I may have underestimated this one.

"I'm sure you are," I murmur.

Zara's breath catches audibly, and her tongue darts out to wet those full lips, leaving them slick and glistening, forcing me to smother a groan.

Zara clears her throat and turns back to the counter. "Anyway, this region is fascinating from a scientific standpoint. The weather patterns are incredibly complex and not well understood."

I grunt, watching her as she works.

Get a grip, I chastise myself sternly. You're the master of your own fate, not some hormonal teen ruled by his cock.

Still, I can't tear my eyes away when Zara bends to slide the quiche into the oven. The dress rides up so far, revealing her panties, and I notice the wet patch right over her cunt. I imagine burying my face there, drinking her arousal, and making her come with my mouth.

"There, that should be ready in about thirty minutes," Zara says, straightening and brushing her hands on a towel.

The movement draws my attention to the flex of her forearms and the delicate bones of her wrists. I can almost feel that fragile skin yielding beneath my calloused grip as I pin her against the wall and—

"Shall we have a seat? I've made a light salad to start." She gestures to the small table.

I blink, forcing my rampant lust back under control with the sheer force of will. One look at her sweet, hopeful expression, and I know there's no way I can act on these twisted urges. I don't know why I fucking care about her expression; I was supposed to murder her, for fuck's sake. Hunt her like an animal, and now look at me?

"Yeah," I manage to grate out. "Let's eat."

Zara beams at me as she takes a seat across from me. My cock can wait—for now, I'll feast on drinking in every detail of her lovely face, committing it to memory. Soon, she'll be screaming my name, writhing beneath me as I take what's mine.

But for this moment, at least, she's untouched by my darkness. Unsullied.

Not for long, little bird. Not for long.

7

ZARA

The next morning, I glance down at the simple dress I just threw on, suddenly feeling self-conscious. The thin cotton clings to my curves, leaving little to the imagination. And I haven't even put on a bra, so my nipples are hard and taut against the fabric.

Should I wear something like this around Aksel?

Yesterday, I thought he was going to fuck me the moment he saw me in a similar dress, although it was maybe a bit more revealing. His intense gaze and desire were palpable, like a living force in the small cabin. I shiver, though not from the chill in the air.

My mind drifts to his powerful physique, those broad shoulders and chiseled features. He's all man—rugged, brooding, and utterly masculine. I've never met anyone like him. The way he moves, the confidence in his stride, the raw power simmering beneath the surface... it's intoxicating.

I can't deny the pull toward him, like a moth drawn to a flame.

What would it be like to finally experience a man's touch? To be claimed and possessed by someone like him?

His bedroom door is closed as I exit my room. After yesterday's tension, I'm a little freaked out, and if I'm honest a little intrigued too. Aksel is raw masculinity, and a part of me wants to explore our connection. Allow him to take control and show me depths of passion I've only ever dreamed about or imagined while I masturbated with my dildo.

At twenty-four years old, being a virgin is rather embarrassing. Still, I guess that's what happens when you spend your life obsessed with science and being a fucking nerd. Guys don't exactly love a woman who won't shut up about weather patterns.

I slip on my rain boots and lightweight jacket, needing to escape the confines of the cabin for a bit. The weight of Aksel's presence and the tension crackling between us is becoming stifling. A short walk may clear my head.

Quietly, I open the cabin door, not wanting to alert Aksel to my departure. The damp forest air caresses my face as I step outside, the drizzling rain leaving a dewy sheen on the surrounding foliage. I pull my hood over my head and head down the narrow dirt path leading away from the cabin.

With each step, I feel the knot in my chest loosening. The sounds of the forest—rustling leaves, distant birdcalls, the steady patter of raindrops—drown out the riot of thoughts swirling in my mind. I focus on the squish of mud beneath my boots, the earthy scent of damp earth.

Rounding a bend, I spot a small clearing up ahead. Sunlight filters through the clouds and canopy and illuminates the vibrant green of the mossy ground. I make my way over, my boots leaving imprints in the spongy terrain. Nestled in the center of the clearing is a large, moss-covered boulder. I clamber up and settle onto the flat surface, crossing my legs and letting the tranquility of this little haven wash over me.

I tilt my face, letting the gentle rainfall kiss my skin. Despite the solitude, I can't shake the feeling of being watched, as if the trees have eyes observing my every move. Is it my overactive imagination playing tricks, or is the forest holding its breath in anticipation?

The snap of a twig somewhere behind me shatters the stillness. I stiffen, my heart pounding as I strain to hear other sounds. Seconds tick by in heavy silence.

Then, another crack of branches, much closer this time. I whip my head around, my breath catching in my throat as I turn to see a wolf staring right at me.

Shit.

My scream pierces the stillness of the forest as the wolf's lips peel back, revealing razor-sharp fangs. A deep, menacing growl rumbles from its throat, raising the hairs on the back of my neck.

"N-Nice doggy," I stammer, sliding off the boulder. My boots hit the mossy ground with a squelch as I back away, hands raised before me.

The wolf steps forward, its piercing amber eyes locked

on me. Another guttural snarl and I can't hold back the whimper that escapes my lips. Panic claws at my chest as the predator stalks closer, its powerful haunches rippling beneath its thick gray fur.

I spin on my heel and bolt, adrenaline propelling me forward. Branches whip at my face as I crash through the forest, not daring to look back. My lungs burn, my heart thunders in my ears, and I race blindly through the forest.

A twisted root catches my foot, and I pitch forward with a cry. The muddy ground rushes up, and I brace myself for the impact, throwing my hands out. Wet leaves and moss cushion my fall, but the wind is still knocked from me in a harsh wheeze.

Gasping, I scramble to get my feet under me, terror lending me strength. Where is the path? Which way is the cabin? My eyes dart frantically between the towering pines surrounding me. Goddamn it. Everything looks the same.

The wolf emerges from the trees, its muzzle wrinkled in a vicious snarl as a growl reverberates through its chest. This is it. I'm going to die here, torn apart by a wild animal in the middle of the Norwegian forest.

The wolf tenses, hind legs gathering beneath it, ready to pounce. I squeeze my eyes shut, bracing for the attack, when a deafening roar shatters the air around us.

My eyes fly open to see Aksel charging toward us, a terrifying sight. He's shirtless, his chiseled torso glistening with rain, tattooed arms bulging with corded muscle. An axe is gripped in one powerful fist.

The wolf falters, ears flattening against its skull as it turns its attention to the threat. Aksel is like a force of nature, power radiating from his imposing frame. He advances with deliberate steps, the axe swinging menacingly at his side.

A warning growl rumbles from the wolf's throat as it analyzes this new adversary. For a breathless moment, the two titans of the forest stare each other down, the air crackling with tension.

Aksel's chest heaves with each breath, raindrops glistening on his tanned skin. His eyes blaze with a primal intensity that makes my heart stutter. He raises the axe slightly, muscles coiling in readiness to strike.

The wolf's lips peel back over its fangs again, and I can't help the whimper that escapes. Please don't let them fight. I can't bear the thought of either one of them getting hurt.

Aksel's head snaps in my direction at the sound, and our eyes lock. His nostrils flare. A fleeting look of concern ghosts across his harsh features before that steely resolve slams back into place.

With a powerful swing of his arm, Aksel hurls the axe. It spins end over end before embedding itself in the ground mere inches from the wolf with a dull thud. The beast startles, letting out a yelp of surprise and dancing back a few paces.

"Leave," Aksel growls, his deep voice laced with quiet menace. "Now."

The wolf's eyes dart between Aksel and the axe. For a tense heartbeat, the great beast appears to weigh its options. Then, with a last look at the both of us, it turns and melts back into the shadowed forest.

The moment the wolf disappears from view, the fight goes out of Aksel. His massive shoulders slump, and he drags a hand down his rain-drenched face with an explosive sigh.

I can't tear my eyes away from Aksel as he strides toward me, the rain sluicing down his sculpted form. His expression is thunderous and his jaw is clenched so tightly the muscle is twitching. But there's also a glimmer of relief flickering in those stormy blue-gray depths.

"What the hell were you thinking wandering off alone like that?" he growls, stopping before me. Despite the anger lacing his words, his hands are remarkably gentle as he grasps my shoulders, giving me a slight shake. "You could've been killed."

I flinch at the intensity blazing in his eyes. The scent of rainwater, musk, and something unmistakably male surrounds me, making my head spin.

"I-I'm sorry," I stammer, feeling impossibly small beneath his smoldering gaze. "I needed some air. I didn't mean to worry you."

One dark brow arches skeptically. "Worry me?" He lets out a low, humorless chuckle, shaking his head. "littlefugl, you terrified me."

My eyes widen at the unexpected admission, and I search his face for any hint of deception. But Aksel's features are an unreadable mask, that tiny flicker of vulnerability already tucked away. Still, I can't ignore the way my heart stumbles over itself at his rare show of emotion.

Seeming to realize how close we're standing, Aksel

drops his hands from my shoulders and steps back, raking a hand through his dripping wet hair. "Just don't wander off again without me, okay?" His tone is gruff but laced with an unmistakable undercurrent of concern. "These woods can be dangerous if you don't know what you're doing. If that wolf had been with a small pack, you'd be torn apart by now, and I wouldn't have been able to save you."

I nod mutely, unable to find my voice beneath the weight of his intense regard. My skin tingles from where his calloused palms gripped me, the memory of his solid warmth searing into me.

"Follow me," he growls, spinning on his heel and leading back toward the cabin.

I trail after him, my steps faltering as I see his broad, muscular back, each flex and ripple of muscle mesmerizing. He's so fucking beautiful.

By the time we reach the cabin door, I'm practically panting, desire and adrenaline swirling in a heady rush. Aksel pauses on the threshold, turning to face me.

"Get inside and dry off," he rumbles, holding my gaze captive with those piercing eyes. "We'll talk once you've warmed up."

I bite the inside of my cheek and don't move. "The storm seems to have cleared. Can't I do some research this afternoon?" I'm eager to get started. Sitting around in a tiny cabin with this man is driving me fucking insane.

I suck in a sharp breath as Aksel's eyes narrow at my request, his expression darkening like a thundercloud rolling in. Tension crackles between us, the air practically sizzling with it.

"You want to go traipsing around the woods again?" he growls, taking a slow, deliberate step toward me. I instinctively shrink back, my heart pounding as that predatory gaze rakes over me. "After nearly becoming a wolf's chew toy?"

Heat rushes to my cheeks, and I bristle at his condescending tone. "I'm not a child who needs to be scolded," I snap, lifting my chin defiantly despite how my pulse races beneath his smoldering stare. "I made a mistake, but I'd like to start my research soon."

Aksel gives a low, rumbling chuckle. He closes the distance between us in two long strides, his imposing frame towering over mine. I track the rivulets of rainwater trailing the cords of muscle on his chest and abdomen.

"You think you can waltz back out there, and everything will be sunshine and wildflowers, littlefugl?" His deep voice is a velvet purr caressing my senses. "The forest is my domain, and I decide when it's safe for you to enter."

I swallow hard, my mouth is suddenly dry as cotton. Aksel's eyes have a gleam that makes me feel utterly exposed, like he can see straight through to the molten desire simmering beneath my skin.

"I-I need to start collecting data soon," I stammer. "If the storm has passed, there's no reason I can't head out for a few hours this afternoon with you as my guide."

Aksel cocks one dark brow, his lips curling into a slow, predatory smile that makes my knees go weak. "You're awfully eager to put yourself in harm's way again, aren't you?" He leans in closer, his woodsy scent surrounding me and making my head spin. "Are you intentionally trying to test me?"

I want to move away, to escape the searing intensity of his stare, but I'm utterly transfixed. Pinned like a butterfly to a board beneath his gaze.

After a long, heated moment, Aksel straightens with a shake of his head. "I'll check the forecast," he rumbles, stepping back and allowing me to draw in a breath. "If it looks clear, I'll decide if you can venture out today. But you'd be wise to prepare yourself for staying put until tomorrow."

My shoulders slump in disappointment, but I know better than to argue. Aksel's tone brooks no debate—he's not asking for my input, merely stating what will happen. A shiver skates down my spine, my core clenching with a strange mix of frustration and arousal.

He holds my gaze for another moment before turning on his heel and striding into the cabin, leaving me flushed and flustered on the porch. I'm mesmerized by the play of his powerful muscles shifting beneath the inked canvas of his back.

I feel that Aksel will keep me under his watchful eye no matter what the forecast says. The thought should terrify me that I'm at the mercy of this intense, unpredictable man.

But a reckless part of me wants nothing more than for him to lock me away in his cabin and have his way with me.

8

AKSEL

My mind races with conflicting desires while I pace the length of my bedroom. The hunger to possess Zara, to mark her as mine, burns through me like an inferno. But an unexpected fear has taken root—the fear that she might come to harm.

I had meticulously planned every detail, determined to hunt her down like a doe and kill her like that wolf would have. And yet, her beauty and innocence are an irresistible lure, tempting me to unleash a different beast.

Clenching my fists, I try to regain control over the swirling storm of emotions. I am the master here, the apex predator. No one dictates my actions or weakens my resolve. And yet...

Zara's defiant spirit and alluring innocence have awoken something primal, something I thought long buried. The need to protect her battles with the urge to defile her, to strip away her purity and claim her as my own.

Growling in frustration, I rake my fingers through my hair. How can one woman disrupt the carefully constructed facade I've built? The plans I had in place and the thrill of the hunt all seem to pale compared to this newfound obsession.

As I continue to pace, my muscles tense with restless energy. The scent of Zara's shampoo, which smells like vanilla and roses, lingers in my nostrils, taunting me with memories of her damp hair clinging to her flushed skin. A low groan escapes my lips as I imagine pinning her beneath me, her cries of pleasure mingling with fearful pleas.

Enough. I need to regain control before this fragile creature unravels me completely. Forcing myself to stillness, I take deep breaths and refocus my thoughts. Zara may have inadvertently awakened something within me, but I will not be undone.

I am the hunter, and she is my prey. Whether I choose to cherish or destroy her remains to be seen.

My cock jerks in my pants, and I realize ignoring it is just making things fucking worse. I haven't masturbated in years. Sex has never been something I'm bothered about. I can take it or leave it, but this girl turns up, and my dick is a fucking steel pole ever since.

I growl in frustration, feeling my cock straining against the confines of my jeans. Enough of this foolishness. I'm in control here, not some raging hormone-addled boy.

Ripping open my belt, I yank down my zipper and free my throbbing dick. The thick shaft pulses in my calloused hand as I give it a firm stroke from base to tip. A guttural groan rumbles from my chest at the much-needed friction.

Bracing one hand against the wall, I lean forward and pump my fist along my rigid cock. Flashes of Zara's flushed cheeks and parted lips invade my mind, stoking the flames. I visualize her on her knees before me, those innocent eyes wide as she takes in the sight of my dick.

"You want this, don't you, littlefugl?" I growl her nickname in Norwegian through gritted teeth, increasing the pace of my strokes. "Beg for it. Beg me to ruin you."

My fantasy Zara whimpers and squirms, torn between fear and wanton need. The thought of defiling her, of marking that flawless skin with my teeth and cum, has me leaking.

Reaching down, I cup my balls and give them a rough squeeze, groaning at the exquisite mix of pleasure and pain. My muscles flex and strain as I chase my release, sweat beading along my brow.

Visions of pinning Zara beneath me, her lithe body writhing as I claim her, push me closer to the edge. I pump my fist furiously, chasing that elusive peak, until finally—

With a feral snarl, I come undone. Hot ropes of cum spurt from my cock, coating the wall and floor in my release. I brace myself on shaking arms, panting harshly when the waves of euphoria crest and ebb.

As the haze of lust clears, I eye the mess I've made with a mixture of disdain and dark amusement. Seems the little bird has more of an effect on me than I'd like. But this was merely a momentary lapse, a way to blow off some steam. I won't allow her to derail me again.

Tucking myself back into my pants, I clean my cum off the floor and wall and then look at myself in the mirror.

"Get it together, Aksel," I coach.

The storm has passed, but I didn't allow Zara to go out today. She won't like it, but after she almost got torn apart by a wolf today, there's no way she's doing any of her research alone. I'll be with her every step of the way.

Convinced I can handle myself tonight and the incessant need satiated, I return to the living room to the delicious scent of food cooking.

Zara is a wonderful cook, as the delicious quiche she made showed. When I get to the kitchen, she's wearing a longer maxi dress that's not so revealing and an apron on, prancing happily around like she belongs here. It's so odd seeing her in my space and not hating it.

I lean against the doorframe, arms folded across my chest, watching. The sway of her hips and the contented smile on her face as she cooks are so domestic—cozy, even. It's a strange sight to behold in my isolated little realm.

"Smells good, littlefugl," I rumble, calling her by my new nickname for her. Little bird in Norwegian.

Zara startles, nearly dropping the spatula in her hand. "Oh! Aksel, you scared me." She presses a hand to her chest, those full lips curving into an embarrassed smile. "I'm just making us some pasta for dinner. I hope you don't mind that I raided your cupboards."

My eyes rake over her appreciatively. "You're welcome to raid anything of mine you'd like."

A delicious blush stains her cheeks at my blatant innuendo. Zara focuses intently on the simmering pot before her. I push off from the doorframe, drawn to her like a fucking magnet.

Prowling up behind her, I let my body heat scorch her back as I crowd her against the counter. A tremor runs through her slight frame when my hands bracket her hips, caging her in.

"You seem right at home here," I murmur, lips brushing her cheek. Zara inhales a shuddering breath, her pulse fluttering.

"A-Aksel…I was just—"

"Shh." I silence her with a firm squeeze of her hips.

Turning her in my arms, I savor her flushed cheeks and full lips. Those green eyes are wide and shining with a heady mix of fear and desire. So beautiful. So tempting.

Reaching up, I brush away a stray lock of golden hair from her face. Zara leans into my touch like a flower seeking the sun, her lush lashes fluttering closed.

"You're playing a dangerous game, little bird," I warn in a low rumble. "Are you sure you want to wake the beast?"

Those emerald eyes open, gleaming with a flash of defiance that has me clenching my jaw. Slowly, deliberately, Zara trails her hands up my chest until they're splayed over my thundering heart.

"And if I do?" she breathes, holding my heated stare. "What then, Mr. Wolf?"

A feral growl rumbles up from my chest as I yank her flush against me. She gasps at the undeniable evidence of my arousal grinding against her belly.

"Then you'll get more than you bargained for, baby girl."

The alarm's shrill beeping slices through the thick tension, jarring us both from the heated moment. Zara jumps away, cheeks flushed and eyes wide like a startled deer. She hurries to remove the steaming pot from the burner with a trembling hand.

I remain rooted in place, chest heaving while I struggle to rein in the raging beast she's awoken. My cock strains painfully against the confines of my jeans.

How is it possible that this slight creature holds such power over me? I had prepared for every eventuality, every twist and turn. Yet, her mere presence derails me in ways I cannot comprehend.

Gritting my teeth, I look away while she busies herself with serving the pasta. I won't be undone by a pair of wide, innocent eyes and a coy smile.

And yet…my body refuses to obey, my cock throbbing insistently. How is it possible to be this ravenous after having just jerked off to climax mere moments ago?

The beast within me snarls, pacing the confines of its cage as I wrestle for control. I had planned to hunt her, to take my time and savor the thrill of the chase. But now? Now, I find myself being pursued, tormented by her every movement.

Zara turns to face me, a hesitant smile curving those full lips. "Dinner's ready," she says softly.

Goddamn it. So tempting, so ripe for the taking.

Slowly, deliberately, I relax my clenched fists and attempt to uncoil the taut muscles that strain for release. I'm the master of my fate, the captain of this storm, and I'll weather it on my own terms.

"Let's eat," I rumble, gesturing for her to sit.

I watch Zara intently as she settles at the table, her every movement sending ripples of desire through my body. The simple act of her lifting the fork to those full lips is enough to have my cock straining.

I focus on the food before me rather than the tempting creature across from me. Each bite is like ash in my mouth as I wrestle with the raging beast clawing at its confines.

Zara appears oblivious to my internal struggle, her delicate brows furrowed in thought as she chews. Those emerald eyes keep flicking to meet my heated stare before shying away.

"Is everything okay?" she asks, finally breaking the weighted silence between us. "You seem tense."

I nearly choke on my next bite at the blatant understatement. Tense doesn't even begin to cover the storm roiling through my veins. Every muscle in my body is coiled tight, aching for release in a way I've never experienced before.

Forcing a smile, I incline my head. "Just fine, littlefugl. Eat your food before it gets cold."

Zara worries her full lower lip, seeming unconvinced. But she obeys nonetheless, turning her attention back to her plate. "What does littlefugl mean?"

I grind my teeth. "Little bird in Norwegian."

Her brow furrows as she meets my gaze. "Why do you call me little bird?" She demands.

So many fucking questions. "No more questions," I growl, "Eat your food."

She does as she's told, and the simple act of submission, no matter how small, has desire flaring hot in my gut. I imagine her kneeling before me, head bowed in deference, as I stroke her golden hair. A shudder wracks my frame at the vivid image, my fork clattering to the plate.

"Aksel?" Zara's soft voice cuts through the haze of lust. "Are you sure you're alright?"

Before I can respond, she reaches across the table to lay her hand atop mine.

The instant Zara's soft hand touches mine, it's like a jolt of electricity shooting straight to my cock. Every nerve ending in my body ignites with a searing need, a primal hunger that leaves me breathless.

Her brow furrows in concern. "What's wrong?"

What's wrong? The words echo in my mind, taunting me with their innocent naivety. If only she knew the dark desires that swirl through me like a tempest, threatening to tear down the carefully constructed walls I've built.

With a herculean effort, I go still, refusing to give in to the beast that claws at its cage. I'm not some lust-crazed animal or a slave to my baser instincts.

Slowly, deliberately, I turn my hand beneath hers until our palms are pressed together. Zara's breath hitches at the intimate contact, her pupils dilating until the green is nearly swallowed by black.

"Nothing is wrong, littlefugl," I rumble. "I'm simply enjoying your company."

A delicate shiver wracks her frame as I brush the pad of my thumb over the skin of her wrist. So soft, so delicate. Like the finest porcelain begging to be marred and broken.

The beast howls its approval, urging me to claim this

tempting creature and ravage her until she's marked with my scent, my essence. But I can't—won't—give in so easily.

With monumental restraint, I disentangle my fingers from hers and sit back in my chair.

Zara blinks rapidly, as if waking from a trance, and quickly withdraws her hand.

An awkward silence stretches between us, thick with tension. I can practically taste the desire in the air, mingling with the lingering scent of her shampoo and driving me half-mad.

Gritting my teeth, I reach for my glass of water and drain it in one burning swallow. The icy liquid does little to quell the inferno raging in my veins and soul.

Zara fidgets across from me, worrying her full lower lip in that delectable way that has me imagining all manner of sinful activities. Unable to bear the weighted silence a moment longer, she clears her throat.

"I should clean up," she murmurs, rising abruptly from the table.

As she moves to gather the dishes, I also find myself rising. Zara freezes as I crowd in behind her for the second time, the plates clattering in her trembling hands. The floral scent of her shampoo envelops me. I inhale deeply, committing that intoxicating aroma to memory.

"Allow me," I rumble, reaching around to still her movements.

My chest presses flush against her back as I loom over her petite frame. Zara's breath comes in shallow pants, her pulse fluttering wildly beneath my fingertips when I brush them over the slender column of her throat. So delicate, so fragile. Like a newborn fawn taking its first, unsteady steps.

I could so easily overwhelm her, crush her against me until she surrendered to the storm raging between us.

"You seem tense, littlefugl," I murmur, allowing my lips to graze the delicate shell of her ear. Zara shivers, her grip tightening on the plates until her knuckles turn white. "Perhaps you need to relax."

Slowly, deliberately, I trail my hands down her arms until I cover hers. I guide her movements, gently prying the dishes from her grip and setting them on the counter.

Zara doesn't protest, doesn't pull away from me. If anything, she melts further into me, her back arching in a way that has me gritting my teeth.

"There, that's better," I rumble, letting my hands linger on her hips. "Wouldn't want you to overexert yourself."

A breathy whimper slips past those full lips as I tease the sensitive skin at the base of her neck with my lips. Zara's head falls back against my shoulder, those emerald eyes slipping closed in silent surrender.

The beast preens at her reaction and how she instinctively bares her throat. It would be so easy to mark that creamy flesh, to sink my teeth into her until she cries out my name in euphoric agony.

Instead, I merely brush my lips over her wildly fluttering pulse point, relishing the full-body shudder that wracks her frame. Zara clutches at my forearms, where they're wrapped around her midriff, silently begging for more.

I finally release her from my embrace and step back with a chuckle, leaving her flushed and trembling against the counter.

"Get some rest," I toss over my shoulder as I head for the living room. "You'll need your energy for tomorrow."

As I settle onto the worn couch, the scent of Zara still clings to me like a heady perfume. Closing my eyes, I commit every hitched breath and whimper to memory. She may have escaped my clutches for now, but the game has only just begun.

The hunt is still on, and my prey has yet to learn how determined her hunter can be.

9

ZARA

I wake with a start, my heart pounding as the scent of fresh pancakes and rich coffee wafts through the cabin. Rubbing the sleep from my eyes, I try to shake off the vivid dreams that plagued me—dreams filled with Aksel's intense gaze and his powerful hands roaming my body.

My stop flips as I recall the way he touched me last night, his fingers and lips making patterns on my neck with a feather-light caress. One minute, he was all heat and barely restrained desire, caging me against the sink. The next, he walked away, telling me to rest before sitting in the living room.

His hot and cold treatment is driving me insane, stoking the fire of want burning low in my belly. I can't deny my magnetic pull toward this wild, unpredictable man. But I know I need to focus—I'm here for research, not to be some rugged Norwegian's plaything.

Forcing my whirling thoughts aside, I throw on a cozy

sweater and a pair of jeans and go to the small kitchen. Aksel stands at the stove, his back to me as he flips a golden pancake. The domestic scene is at odds with the raw, predatory energy that crackles around him.

Clearing my throat, I give him a tentative smile as he turns to face me. "Morning. Those pancakes smell amazing."

He turns to me, his lips quirk in a half-smirk that makes my heart flutter. "Morning, little bird. Hungry?"

I nod, unable to find my voice as his heated gaze rakes over me. Grabbing a plate, I load it with the fluffy pancakes.

I sit and pour myself a mug of coffee, eating and trying to ignore the brooding Norwegian.

"Are you ready for your first hike? I will accompany you since it's too dangerous to go alone," he says, breaking through the silence.

I plaster my brightest smile, determined not to let Aksel rattle me. "Of course, I'm excited for you to join me! The more the merrier."

His eyes narrow as if he can see right through my cheerful facade. I hold his intense gaze, refusing to let him shake my resolve. I may be drawn to this man in a way I can't quite explain, but I won't let him intimidate me.

"Wonderful." His deep voice sends a shiver down my spine. "We'll leave after breakfast. Dress warmly, littlefugl. The Norwegian air can be unforgiving."

I give a firm nod, focusing on clearing my plate. The pet name rolls off his tongue so easily, both endearing and possessive. I shouldn't like that this stranger has given me a nickname, and I know I should tell him not to call me it to establish healthy boundaries. However, I like it when he calls me it.

Shoving that dangerous thought aside, I rise and rinse my dishes. "I'll go get ready then. Thank you for breakfast. It was delicious."

His eyes burn into my back as I head for the bedroom to add more layers. I can feel the heat of his stare like a physical caress. Grabbing my warmest clothes, I quickly strip and redress, my movements efficient. There is no need to linger and let my mind wander to inappropriate places.

Once bundled up in thermal leggings, a thick sweater, and sturdy hiking boots, I return to the living room. Aksel stands by the door, looking every bit the rugged mountain man in his heavy coat and boots.

He gives me an approving once-over that has my cheeks flushing. "Ready?"

"Ready," I confirm, grabbing my pack and equipment and following him into the crisp mountain air. As we start down the trail, I can't help stealing glances at the powerful man leading the way.

This is going to be a long, torturous hike, but I can't deny the thrill of excitement that courses through me when I think about spending the day alone with Aksel in the wilderness.

"So, how long have you lived up here?" I ask, aiming for a breezy tone to cover my nerves.

Aksel remains silent, his boots crunching on the rocky path as we hike deeper into the forest. I press on undeterred, determined not to let his stoic demeanor get me down. "It's just so beautiful and peaceful. I can see why you'd want to escape it here."

He shoots me a sidelong glance, one dark brow raised as if amused by my rambling. I give him my sunniest smile, refusing to be intimidated.

"You know, when I was a little girl, I always dreamed of visiting Norway," I continue, stepping beside him. "My dad used to tell me stories about the Vikings and their adventures. I was fascinated by their fearlessness, their ability to conquer any challenge through sheer force of will."

I pause, gauging his reaction. His expression remains unreadable, but a glint in his eye makes me think he's listening intently despite his silence.

Emboldened, I go on. "Of course, those were just childhood fantasies. I never imagined seeing this incredible country with my own eyes one day. The reality is so much more breathtaking than I could have dreamed."

I stop, struck by the sheer majesty of the mountains looming ahead of us, the dense pines swaying gently in the breeze. A serene smile curves my lips as I take it all in. "Isn't it just magnificent?"

Aksel follows my gaze, his expression unreadable as ever. For a long moment, the only sound is the crunch of our boots on the trail. When I think he will remain stubbornly silent, he speaks in that deep, rumbly tone that sends shivers down my spine.

"Yes, little bird. The mountains hold a raw, untamed power that most people cannot comprehend." His eyes find mine, pinning me in place with their intensity. "It's a force to be reckoned with that demands respect and complete submission."

A thrill runs through me at the word "submission". Swallowing hard, I force a bright smile. "Well, I'm certainly looking forward to getting better acquainted with Norway's wild side," I tease, trying to downplay the tension between us.

Aksel's lips curve in a wolfish grin that has my heart stuttering. "I've no doubt you are, little bird. No doubt at all."

With that, he turns and continues along the trail, leaving me scurrying to catch up.

Once we get to a clearing, I clear my throat. "This spot is perfect," I announce, setting my pack down and unzipping it to retrieve my equipment.

Aksel watches me as I unpack the sensors and instruments I need to monitor atmospheric conditions. My hands are steady and sure, and the familiar routine calms my nerves after our hike's heated tension.

"I'll need to set up the anemometer to measure wind speed and direction," I explain, not caring if he's listening. Talking through my process is as much for my own benefit as his.

I move about the small clearing, carefully positioning the device and securing it to the ground with the metal stakes. Once calibrated, I make a few notes in my field book, recording the time and location.

Next, I pull out the digital thermometer and psychrometer to gauge air temperature and humidity levels. These require more maneuvering to properly elevate them off the ground and shield them from direct sunlight per protocol.

All the while, I can feel the weight of Aksel's stare boring into me. He hasn't said a word, but his presence is a tangible force, commanding my attention even as I focus on my work. I refuse to let him rattle me, keeping my movements professional.

Once the rest of my sensors are in place, I straighten and brush my hands on my thighs, surveying my setup with a satisfied nod. "Okay, I'll need to let these run for a while to get a solid data sample. Then we can move to the next site."

I turn to find him watching me with an inscrutable expression, his eyes gleaming like a predator studying its prey. A delicious shiver runs down my spine, and I hold his smoldering gaze, refusing to be the first to break it.

"Is there anything else I can help with while we wait?" His deep voice reverberates through me, awakening the simmering want I've been trying to ignore since I got here two days ago.

I open my mouth to reply, but my words catch in my throat as he stalks toward me with the lethal grace of a panther. My heart is pounding with every step he takes, closing the distance between us until his powerful form dwarfs mine completely.

"Or perhaps..." He reaches out to toy with a loose strand of my hair, his calloused fingers brushing my cheek ever so lightly. "You could use a break, little bird?"

His words are low and gravelly, laced with an undeniable heat that has arousal blooming between my thighs. I should pull away and remind him I'm here for research, not whatever this dangerous game is between us.

But I can't bring myself to move or tear my gaze away from the molten promise blazing in his eyes. I'm utterly enthralled, caught in the spell of his raw masculinity.

My lips part on a shaky exhale as he leans in closer, the faint scent of pine and musk surrounding me. This close, I can see the flecks of gray in his hooded eyes. My fingers itch with the urge to reach out and touch him, finally sate the growing ache inside me.

"Well?" His breath ghosts over my lips, making me shudder. "What shall it be, little bird?"

10

AKSEL

I stare at Zara, my arms wrapped tightly around her. Her eyes are wide with a mixture of curiosity and apprehension. "What do you mean?"

Everything about her should make me despise her. She talks too fucking much, and she's always so annoyingly happy, even in this godforsaken wilderness.

"Aksel?" Her delicate fingers graze my cheek, snapping me back to reality. "Are you okay?"

I don't answer, lost in the depths of her green eyes. Despite her incessant cheerfulness, something about her draws me in. Perhaps it's the contrast—her light to my darkness, her innocence to my depravity. They do say opposites attract.

"Aksel?" she prompts again, her brow furrowed with concern.

I've never considered sharing my life with anyone. The mere thought of letting someone in, of exposing my true self, has always filled me with revulsion. And yet, as I gaze upon this little bird's angelic face, I find myself yearning to do that. To share every twisted desire, every dark craving, with the one person who might understand. Who might accept me for the monster I am.

Tearing my gaze away from her captivating eyes, the spell is momentarily broken. I clear my throat. "I'm fine." The lie rolls off my tongue with practiced ease, and I release her from my hold.

Zara's brow is still creased with concern. "You seemed distant for a moment there." She chews her plump lower lip, and I can't help but imagine how those soft lips would feel pressed against mine.

Shaking my head to dispel the intrusive thought, I smile reassuringly. "Just got lost in thought, that's all." My fingers itch to reach out and smooth the worry lines from her forehead to trace the delicate curve of her jaw. But I resist the urge, clenching my fists at my sides.

"If you're sure…" Zara's gaze lingers on me for a heartbeat longer before she turns away, busying herself with her equipment.

I watch her movements, mesmerized by the gentle sway of her hips and how the sunlight catches in her golden hair. Every fiber of my being screams at me to close the distance, to pull her lithe body flush against mine and claim her out here in the open.

But I need to maintain control. Because once I've tasted the forbidden fruit, I know there'll be no turning back. She'll consume me, body and soul until nothing remains but the insatiable hunger for her.

So, for now, I'm content with drinking in the sight of her, committing every curve to memory. Zara doesn't realize it yet, but she's already mine—a delicate butterfly caught in the spider's web, destined to be slowly, exquisitely devoured.

After tinkering for about half an hour, she smiles sweetly at me. "We're ready to move higher up the mountain for more readings."

She packs her equipment back in her pack and shoulders it.

I grind my teeth. "That looks heavy. Do you want me to carry it for the next leg?" After all, I'm stronger than her, and it'll be easy.

Her smile practically kills me. "That's so kind of you. It would help. My back is killing me. I'm not used to hiking."

Grunting in response to mask my eagerness to assist her, I slide the pack from her shoulders and sling it over my own with deft movements. The weight is nothing, but I relish the way her eyes widen slightly at the flex of my biceps.

"Thanks, Aksel," she breathes, flushing. "I really appreciate it."

A grin tugs at the corners of my mouth. "Don't mention it, littlefugl."

Turning on my heel, I lead the way up the narrow trail, maintaining a leisurely pace that allows Zara to keep up. I glance over my shoulder every so often, savoring how her chest heaves with exertion, the sheen of perspiration that glistens on her skin.

After a particularly steep incline, she pauses to catch

her breath, one hand braced against the trunk of a towering pine. "Mind if we take a break?" she pants, swiping a loose tendril of hair from her flushed face.

"Of course not." I lean casually against a tree a short distance away, allowing my gaze to roam shamelessly over every shapely curve of her body. "We're in no hurry."

Zara shoots me a sidelong glance. She knows the effect she has on me—how could she not when I make no effort to conceal my desire? And yet, rather than shrinking away, she holds my stare, her plump lower lip caught between her teeth.

This little bird may flutter and trill, but she knows her place deep down. She knows that she belongs to me, body and soul.

Pushing off from the tree, I eat up the distance between us. Zara's breath hitches as I loom over her, caging her against the rough bark with my arms braced on either side of her head.

"Do you have any idea what you do to me?" I murmur. Without waiting for a response, I dip my head to whisper into her ear. "The things I want to do to you?"

A tremor courses through her slight frame, and I inhale deeply, savoring her intoxicating scent. My tongue darts out to trace the curve of her ear, and she whimpers, her nails digging into the bark at her back.

"Aksel..." It's a plea, and I revel in the desperation laced through that single, breathless utterance.

Pulling back to meet her wide gaze, I offer her a feral grin. "Don't worry," I purr, my fingers trailing down to ghost over the swell of her breasts. "Not here, baby girl," I murmur against the skin of her throat.

Zara's pulse flutters rapidly beneath my lips, and I can't resist nipping at the delicate column of her neck, loving the way she gasps and arches against me.

Every nerve screams to take what I want—to claim this sweet, tempting creature. Her scent of vanilla and roses alone makes me ache to defile her.

With a low growl, I capture her wrists and pin them above her head, drinking in the sight of her at my mercy. "You've got no idea how badly I want you, littlefugl." My voice is a guttural rasp as I grind my hips against hers, allowing her to feel how hard I am.

Zara whimpers, her eyes fluttering shut as her hips move upward in a desperate bid for friction. "Please..." The breathless plea falls from her parted lips.

Leaning in, I allow my lips to brush against the corner of her mouth, a mere ghost of a kiss that has her straining against my hold. "You want this?" I murmur, my tongue tracing the seam of her lips in a silent demand for entry. "You want me to take you right here, in the heart of the wilderness?"

Her only response is a needy whine, her body arching as she seeks the friction I so cruelly deny her. Desire courses through my veins like liquid fire, and it's all I can do to maintain my tenuous grip on control.

With a frustrated growl, I tear my lips from the temptation of her mouth, panting harshly as I force myself to pull back. "As much as I want to claim you here and now, we can't risk it." My voice is strained, gravelly with the effort of reining in my baser instincts. "It'll be dark soon, and we must return before nightfall."

Zara's eyes flutter open, hazy with lust and confusion. "But...I thought..." Her brow furrows adorably as she struggles to formulate a coherent thought.

I trace the delicate line of her jaw with the pad of my thumb. "Oh, don't worry. I've no intention of denying myself any longer. But we need to make it back to the safety of the cabin first. After that..." I lean in to nip at the tender flesh below her ear. "All bets are off."

I force myself to remove my lips from her skin with a monumental effort. "Now, let's hike to the next spot and get your data before returning." I ensure my voice is casual and calm despite not feeling in control.

I continue up the mountain trail, Zara's pack slung effortlessly over my shoulder.

The silence between us is charged and electric, neither daring to break it. Zara trails a few paces behind me, her gaze fixed resolutely on the ground before her. Gone is the incessant chatter, the cheerful demeanor that grated on my nerves. In its place is a palpable tension that has my blood thrumming hotly in my veins.

Reaching the next vantage point, I turn to face her. "Here's a good spot."

Zara starts at my voice, her gaze snapping to meet mine. In that single, heated glance, I see the conflict within her—the war between the innocent little bird and the wanton creature I've awoken. Her teeth worry at her plump lower lip, and I have to clench my fists to keep from closing the distance between us and claiming that tempting mouth with bruising intensity.

"R-right," she stammers, moving toward me to retrieve her pack before busying herself with her equipment.

I watch in silence as she works, my eyes tracing the delicate curve of her throat and the gentle swell of her breasts beneath the thin fabric of her shirt. Every movement, every subtle shift of her body, has me aching to pin her against the nearest surface and bury myself in her cunt.

After a few agonizing minutes, Zara straightens. I've got everything set up. It'll be half an hour to collect all the data," she murmurs, her voice a breathless whisper.

"Understood," I rumble, my gaze devouring every inch of her. The knowledge that she'll be standing here, within arm's reach for the next half hour, is almost more than I can bear.

Zara shifts her weight from one foot to the other. She opens her mouth as if to speak but seems to think better of it, snapping her jaw shut with an audible click.

The silence that stretches between us is thick and charged. I can practically taste the tension in the air, as palpable as the crisp mountain breeze that ruffles my hair.

Forcing my features into a mask of casual indifference, I lean back against the trunk of a nearby tree and fold my arms across my chest. The movement draws Zara's gaze like a moth to a flame, her eyes darkening as they trace the flex of my inked biceps.

A low chuckle rumbles in my chest, and I watch in silent satisfaction as her blush deepens. "See something you like?"

She holds my stare for a long, heated moment, her eyes shining with a mix of want and uncertainty.

Then, as if remembering herself, she tears her gaze away. "I...I should get back to work," she murmurs breathlessly.

I hum in acknowledgment before pushing off from the tree and prowling closer, savoring the way Zara's breath catches in her throat. "By all means," I purr, leaning in close. "Don't let me distract you."

Forcing myself to step back, I offer Zara a wolfish grin. "I'll just be over here watching."

Her cheeks flush an even deeper shade of crimson. For a moment, it seems as though she might protest, might demand that I give her space to work.

But then, something shifts in her gaze—a glimmer of defiance, of challenge. Squaring her delicate shoulders, she holds my stare, her chin tilting up in a wordless show of bravado.

A low growl rumbles in my chest as I drink at the sight of her newfound boldness.

Sinking down onto a nearby boulder, I stretch out my legs and make a show of getting comfortable while holding Zara's gaze with a heated intensity that leaves no doubt as to my intentions.

The game is afoot, and I'm a patient hunter, content to wait for the perfect moment to strike. Zara may put on a brave face, but we both know that she is utterly, inescapably mine. It's only a matter of time before the hunt reaches its inevitable, delicious conclusion.

Until then, I'm more than happy to savor every heated

glance, every breathless gasp. The anticipation is half the thrill, after all.

So I watch and wait, secure in the knowledge that by the night's end, my sweet little bird will be thoroughly, irrevocably claimed.

11

ZARA

I rush into my bedroom, slamming the door behind me and pushing the bolt across. My heart is pounding so hard I can hear the blood rushing in my ears.

What the hell am I thinking?

Aksel is the most powerfully built, ruggedly handsome man I've ever seen. It's only natural I'm insanely attracted to him. But there's something unhinged about my host—something dark and dangerous lurking under the surface that I should run far away from.

Yet a traitorous part of me wants him to claim me, to introduce me to pleasures I couldn't even dream of. To finally, mercifully, rid me of this utterly embarrassing virginity at my age.

I shake my head, trying to dislodge the wanton thoughts. Stripping off my hiking gear, I toss it in the corner and purposefully dress in my most unappealing, frumpy clothes. A pair of baggy sweatpants and a loose, shapeless top. Anything to dampen Aksel's interest and my own arousal.

A heavy fist pounds on the door. "Zara? You okay in there?"

Aksel's deep voice slices through me like a hot knife. I shiver, hugging myself. "Y-Yes, I'm fine! Just changing."

There's a pause, then, "Don't make me come in there, baby girl."

The blatant threat in his tone makes my breath catch. I can picture his eyes narrowing, jaw clenched with impatience when I defy him. Taking a deep, steadying breath, I open the door. Aksel is leaning against the opposite wall, arms crossed over his chest. His eyes instantly rake over me from head to toe.

Despite the shapeless, unflattering clothes I'm wearing, his gaze darkens. It's as if he can see right through the fabric to my naked body underneath.

Heat blooms across my cheeks as I avert my eyes. "I've got to check over the data I collected."

Aksel pushes off the wall, stalking toward me. I instinctively back up until I'm flattened against the door frame.

He towers over me, so close I can smell the intoxicating blend of fresh pine, motor oil, and sheer masculinity. His eyes bore into mine with an intensity that made me feel stripped bare.

"You can try to hide that gorgeous body all you want, littlefugl," he rumbles, the Norwegian endearment rolling off his tongue. "But you can't hide the desire in your eyes when you look at me."

His calloused finger traces the curve of my jaw, raising

goosebumps across my skin. I shiver, unable to tear my gaze away from his.

"I see how you react to me," Aksel murmurs, leaning in until his lips graze my ear. "I can sense your arousal every time I'm near you. It calls to me."

I can't stop the whimper that escapes my lips as his words send molten heat pooling between my thighs. This man has an otherworldly power over me that I can't resist, no matter how hard I try.

"I've made Lapskaus. It's a beef stew. I hope you're hungry."

I blink rapidly, trying to process Aksel's abrupt subject change. One minute, he's practically undressing me with his eyes and whispering sinful things; the next, he's talking about...beef stew?

A confused frown tugs at my lips as I nod slowly. "Uh, yeah. Lapskaus sounds great."

I clear my throat, attempting to gather my composure and revert back to my usual cheerful self. Squaring my shoulders, I offer him a bright smile. "I'm starving after that hike. I can't wait to dig in!"

Aksel's gaze doesn't waver as he studies me carefully. I resist the urge to squirm under his scrutiny. "Good," he rumbles. "You'll need to keep your energy up for later."

The insinuation in his words causes heat to creep into my cheeks. I open my mouth to respond, but he's already turning on his heel and heading back toward the kitchen.

Left alone, I exhale a shaky breath. *Get it together, Zara. He's just trying to fluster you.*

Pushing off the door frame, I follow the mouthwatering aroma of stew wafting from the kitchen. Aksel is bent over the pot on the stove, stirring the contents.

I quickly avert my eyes before he catches me ogling him. Again. Clearing my throat, I take a seat at the rustic old table. "It smells amazing. I didn't realize you were such a good cook."

Aksel casts me a sidelong glance over his shoulder, one corner of his sensuous mouth quirking up. "There's a lot you don't know about me."

I tuck a loose strand of hair behind my ear. "Well, maybe you can enlighten me over dinner then."

His darkening gaze sweeps brazenly over my body once more before returning to the stew. "Maybe I will."

Despite my attempt to downplay the sizzling tension, I know there's no denying the primal attraction that crackles between us. I worry my lower lip, unable to shake the feeling that I may be in over my head with this man. Yet that only seems to excite me more.

Aksel ladles hearty portions into two bowls. He sets one in front of me with a grunt before taking the seat across the table.

"This looks incredible," I gush, hoping some enthusiastic conversation will help dissipate the tension. "I don't think I've ever had authentic Norwegian cuisine."

Aksel merely gives a noncommittal shrug as he digs into his food. I study his chiseled features, trying to read his stony expression. His dark brows are furrowed in their usual brooding scowl.

Undeterred, I forge ahead with the small talk. "So, will

you tell me how long you've lived out here? In this cabin, I mean."

He pauses, meeting my gaze with those intense eyes that never fail to make my breath catch. "Long enough."

I fidget in my seat, nodding slowly. "Right, of course. It's really...cozy. Rustic."

An awkward silence stretches between us as we eat. I sneak glances at Aksel, admiring the sharp angles of his jaw, the smattering of dark stubble, and the intriguing ink of his tattoos peeking from beneath the sleeves of his shirt.

Clearing my throat, I try again. "Those are really cool tattoos, by the way. What do they mean?"

His eyes narrow slightly as he regards me. For a moment, I think he will brush me off again. But then he slowly rolls up his sleeve, revealing an intricate pattern of symbols twisting around his muscular forearm.

"Norse runes," he rumbles. "Protection symbols. Strength. Guides for journeys."

"Wow," I breathe, leaning closer to get a better look. I can't resist reaching out to lightly trace the swirling black lines with my fingertip. "They're beautiful."

Aksel turns deathly still, holding my captive gaze as I continue trailing over the ink. A heavy intensity simmering in his eyes causes my heart to slam against my ribs.

"You find them intriguing?" he murmurs, voice taking on a deep, gravelly quality.

Heat prickles along my neck as I give a shaky nod. "V-Very. I've always been fascinated by ancient cultures and symbolism."

A smirk tugs at the corner of Aksel's mouth, crinkling the laugh lines around his eyes. "Is that so?"

I swallow hard, my fingers stilling on his arm. Electricity seems to spark between us, raising the fine hairs along my skin. "Maybe you could tell me more about them some time?"

The words come out in a breathless whisper as my gaze moves to his lips. Full and sensuous, I can't help imagining how they might feel against mine.

"Maybe I will, littlefugl," Aksel rumbles. "If you ask nicely."

I can barely choke down another bite of the delicious stew. My mouth has gone so dry. The tension has become suffocating, charging the air with an electric current.

As he finishes the last few bites, Aksel pushes his empty bowl aside and stands in one fluid motion. My breath catches as he moves to stand behind me. The heat of his solid body radiates against my back, making me hyperaware of every inch of space between us.

Aksel leans down until his lips graze the shell of my ear. His stubble scratches my sensitive skin as he murmurs in a low, dangerous rumble, "I'm done playing games."

A shudder races down my spine at the blatant threat in his tone. This is it—he's finally making his move. Part of me has been anticipating this moment with a heady mixture of fear and arousal. But now that it's here, panic surges through my veins.

"I-I'm a virgin!" I blurt out, instantly regretting the words.

He goes rigid against me for a beat. Then, a rumbling

chuckle vibrates against my back as he presses closer, caging me against the table. "Is that so?"

I give a shaky nod, my pulse thundering in my ears. "Y-Yes. I've never...I mean, I don't have any experience..."

"Shhh." He soothingly brushes my hair aside, baring the slender column of my throat. His lips hover a hairsbreadth away as he growls, "That's nothing to be ashamed of, baby girl. In fact..."

Aksel's large, calloused hand slides around to boldly cup my breast through my baggy top. I gasp sharply at the intimate contact as he kneads my breast with firmness.

"It just means I'll have to be extra gentle when I claim what's mine," he rasps against my neck. "When I take my time ruining you for any other man."

Arousal slams into me with dizzying force. My thighs clench instinctively as slick heat pools between them. This man has awakened something I didn't even know existed inside me until now.

"You want that, don't you?" Aksel's teeth graze along the sensitive skin just below my ear. "You want me to take my time stripping away every last shred of your innocence?"

I can only nod helplessly, rendered mute by the overwhelming sensations assaulting me. His free hand tangles in my hair, angling my head to allow his lips to blaze a scorching path along the column of my throat.

"Then you'll do as I say," he commands in a rough growl. "You're mine now, littlefugl. And I will make sure you never forget who you belong to."

12

AKSEL

Goddamn it.

A virgin. A fucking virgin.

How is this possible? This beautiful, chatty, and happy little creature has never been fucked. And now it means we're both utterly screwed. Once I have her, she's mine forever. There will be no going back.

"Aksel, please," she moans.

I force her chair around and lean in, crushing my mouth to hers. Her lips are so soft, pliant, and she tastes like fucking sunshine. I've never kissed a woman like this. I want to devour her, claim her, own her. She whimpers against my mouth, and it sends a shock straight to my cock.

Breaking the kiss, I stand and pull her up from the chair, lifting her into my arms. She doesn't weigh a thing, and I carry her easily; her legs wrap around my waist.

"Aksel," she breathes, her eyes glassy with desire.

I step toward the back room of my cabin and carry her into the hunting room which is dark and cool and smells of leather and earth. I kick the door shut behind us and set her down, keeping one hand on her waist to steady her.

"You're so beautiful," I mutter, my voice low. I can't take my eyes off her. She's perfect, her skin flushed, her lips red and swollen from my kiss.

She bites her lip, and it takes all my control not to tear her clothes off and destroy her.

"Take off your top," I order, unable to keep the edge of demand from my voice. I want to see all of her.

Her hands tremble as she lifts the top over her head. I step back, taking in the reveal of her skin, the lacy edges of a black bra that does nothing to hide the swell of her breasts.

Fuck. This woman is going to be the end of me. I want to brand her, mark her as mine. I ball my hands into fists, digging my short nails into my palms, fighting the need to touch.

She's fucking gorgeous. My free hand reaches out, tracing the curve of her waist, then up, following the line of her ribs until I cup her breast through the bra before reaching around and unhooking it. It falls to the floor, and I hiss in a breath at the sight of her breasts. Her skin is so soft, and she fits perfectly in my hand. I thumb her nipple, now tight and peaked, and she gasps, her head falling back.

"You like that, don't you?" I don't wait for an answer. Instead, I lean down, my mouth replacing my hand. She tastes even better than she looks.

I step back, watching as she shivers, goosebumps rising on her bare skin. "Take off the rest," I growl.

Her eyes, wide and glassy, flick down to my mouth, then back up. She bites her lip, and my cock twitches. Slowly, she reaches down, hooking her thumbs into the waistband of her jogging pants.

"Go on," I urge.

Her breath hitches as she strips, kicking off her pants and underwear together. And fuck, she's beautiful. My dick is aching, throbbing with the need to be inside her, but I force myself to hold back. This is a moment to savor.

I let my eyes roam over her body, taking in the curve of her hip, the swell of her breasts, and the way her stomach dips in. She's fucking perfect.

Then, still keeping my distance, I reach for one of my knives, enjoying how her eyes widen; a mix of fear and excitement flashes across her face.

"Aksel?" she asks, her voice shaking.

I smile, showing her the knife. "I'm not going to hurt you, littlefugl. Well, not much anyway." I step closer, backing her against the wall, tracing the flat side of the knife up her inner thigh. "This is for your pleasure."

She tries to turn, but I grab her waist, holding her still. "Trust me," I murmur against her mouth. "You're going to like this."

Her breath catches as I drag the knife back down, pressing the tip just hard enough to leave a pink line.

"See?" I whisper, pressing a kiss to her neck.

She nods, and I draw the knife back up, slower this time, dragging it across her soft skin. She whimpers, her head falling back to give me access to the sensitive skin of her throat.

I keep one hand on her waist, the other tracing the knife over her body, careful to avoid any sensitive spots. The blade teases and elicits little gasps and moans from her, her body jerking with each touch.

Then, setting the knife aside, I trace the marks I've left with my tongue, tasting her, claiming her.

"Aksel, please," she whimpers, her hands reaching for me. "I want to see you."

I groan, my cock twitching. I know what she means. I want her to see me, too. With a rough laugh, I step back, already unbuttoning my shirt.

"You sure about this, baby girl? There's no going back." I warn, needing her to understand the gravity of this moment.

"I'm sure," she says, her voice steady, and something in her eyes tells me she gets it. She knows this is a point of no return, that we're stepping into something we can't take back.

I strip off my shirt, enjoying how her eyes take in the tattoos covering my skin. Her gaze fixes on the ink, and I know she's curious, wanting to know the stories they hold. But that's for another time.

With a slow, deliberate movement, I reach for the button of my jeans, my eyes never leaving hers. There's a challenge in her gaze as if she's daring me to go further, but also a hint of fear.

The button pops open, and I lower the zipper, my cock

straining against the denim. Her breath catches, and her eyes are fixed on the bulge.

Finally, I push my jeans and underwear down, kicking them aside, and step toward her, fully exposed. Her eyes drop to my cock, and her mouth falls open. I know what she's thinking. I'm fucking huge, and the thought of me filling her tight little body, stretching her, drives me fucking wild.

"Oh," she gasps, her hand flying to her mouth. "You're..."

I chuckle, already knowing what she's going to say. "Yeah, I know. It's a lot to take in, baby girl. But don't worry, I'll go slow."

Her eyes snap back to mine. "I want you, Aksel."

"You may not say that when you realize what that means, but for your first time, I won't introduce you to my true nature." I want to hunt her still, just in a completely different way from how I originally planned. My blood lust is replaced with a deeper, more carnal lust.

I grab a fistful of her hair, relishing the little gasp it elicits. "You sure you're ready for this?" I growl, angling her head back to meet my gaze. "I like it rough. Real rough and primal. You sure that's what you want?"

Her eyes are bright with desire, and she nods, licking her lips. "Yes. I think so."

Fuck, those words go straight to my cock. I can already tell she'll be a little freak in bed, responsive and vocal. My blood is boiling with the need to take her, to hear her scream my name.

I lift her easily, her legs wrapping around my waist as I

carry her to the nearby bench. Setting her down, I push her back to lie on the cool wood, her hair spilling over the edge. She looks up at me, her eyes glassy with anticipation, and I can't help but smirk.

"You've got no idea what you're in for, littlefugl."

Reaching for my knife, I imagine all the ways I can mark her, possess her. But first, I need a taste.

I step between her legs, already spread wide for me, and trace the flat of the blade up her inner thigh, enjoying the way she squirms. "You like the feel of this, don't you?"

She nods, her breath coming in short gasps. "Yes."

I drag the blade closer to her core, making her breath hitch. "That's it. Give in."

But then I move the knife aside and use my fingers to gently part her folds. She's fucking gorgeous, all pink and swollen, and I can't resist. I lean down, my tongue flicking out to taste her, and she jerks underneath me with a gasp.

She's fucking addictive. I can't get enough. I lick and suck, gripping her thighs to hold her open while her breath comes in short sharp gasps. Her hands grasp at my head, trying to hold me there.

I enjoy how her fingers tangle in my hair, and she pulls at it, her body arching off the table. I force myself to keep a slow, steady rhythm with my tongue despite her whimpers and moans driving me insane.

I use my tongue and teeth to play with her, nipping gently, then soothing it with soft sucks. Her hips buck, trying to get more pressure. I chuckle, the vibrations making her squirm.

"Not yet, littlefugl. I haven't given you permission."

I shift, moving my mouth to suck gently on her clit, my fingers replacing my tongue, circling and pressing, my thumb rubbing little circles around her entrance. She's so wet, her juices coating my fingers, and I slip one inside, enjoying the way she moans and arches into my touch.

"Aksel, please," she begs, her hips grinding against my hand.

I add a second finger, scissoring them and stretching her, feeling her tight heat. She's so fucking responsive, her body trembling with each touch, and I know she's hovering on the edge. But I can't let her fall just yet.

Slowing my movements, I drag my mouth away, enjoying the little whimper of protest she makes. I smirk, reaching for the knife again, and trace it gently up her thigh, not pressing hard enough to cut but enough to make her shiver.

"You like that, don't you?" I murmur. "You like the feel of the blade, the danger of it."

She nods, her eyes glassy and unfocused. "Yes, I like it. I like everything you're doing."

Fuck, this woman is going to be my downfall.

"Before you come apart, I want you to taste me."

Her mouth, those lips, will be the end of me. I can't stop thinking about them wrapped around my cock, sucking me in, taking me deep.

I need it now.

Grabbing a handful of her hair, I drag her off the bench, feeling her small body yield as I force her to her knees. She looks at me, her eyes wide and glassy, and my dick twitches with anticipation.

"Suck me, baby girl," I growl, stepping closer. "Wrap that pretty little mouth around my cock."

She hesitates, her eyes darting to my dick and back up, and something tells me she's never done this before. Fuck. I want to be her first in everything.

"You ever sucked a cock before?" I ask.

She shakes her head. "No, I haven't. I--I've never--"

"It's okay, you can't do it wrong." I urge, needing to feel her mouth on me. "Just put your lips around me and suck."

She nods, her hands reaching out as if to steady herself. Slowly, she leans forward, her tongue flicking out to tentatively taste the head of my dick. Fuck, the feel of her tongue makes me want to thrust into her throat.

"That's it," I encourage, my hands tangling in her hair. "Take me in."

She opens her mouth wider, and I guide myself to her lips, sliding into her hot, wet mouth. She takes me, inch by inch, her eyes closed in concentration.

The sight of her, my cock disappearing between her lips, is enough to make my knees weak. I've never felt anything like it, and I want to thrust, to fuck her throat, but I force myself to hold still, giving her time to adjust.

"That's it," I groan. "Fucking take me deep, littlefugl."

She makes a little moaning noise, and I start to thrust gently, her throat enveloping me, hot and tight. Her tongue swirls around me, and her teeth drag against me, just a hint of sharpness that drives me wild.

"You're doing so good, baby girl," I praise, my hips moving slightly faster. "Suck me like you mean it."

Her hands clutch at my thighs, her mouth working me,

and I can feel my control slipping. This girl is going to be my undoing, but damn if I don't love every second of it.

I start to thrust harder, faster, my hips moving with a rhythm that has her making little gagging noises. Tears spill down her cheeks, and saliva spills down her chin. Goddamn, it's the hottest thing I've ever seen. Her mouth is pure fucking sin, and I know I won't last long.

"That's it," I groan, my eyes closing as I savor the sensation. "Fuck, you're so good."

I can feel my orgasm building, coiling tight in my stomach, and I know I'm not going to last much longer.

Forcing myself to stop, I know what I need next. Zara's tight little cunt is wrapped around me, feeling her muscles squeeze me as I fuck her. But first, I want to show her my darkness.

Growling, I yank her to her feet, pressing her back against the table. She makes a little noise of surprise, and her eyes go wide when she feels my cock pressing against her cunt.

My hands grip her hips. "You like the feel of my cock?"

"Yes. Oh God, yes."

"Tell me what you want. Beg for it." My voice is rough, my need for her making me primal.

"I want you to fuck me," she breathes, her voice shaking. "Please. I need you inside me."

Fuck, her words send a jolt of desire straight to my cock. I want to tear her open with my need, claim her so thoroughly that she can never forget who she belongs to.

I reach for my knife, the one I used to tease and torment her before. But this time, I'm not going to be gentle. This time, I will show her the darkness that lives within.

I press the blade to her throat, relishing the way she gasps, her body going still. "You want me to fuck you, baby girl? You sure about that?"

She nods, her eyes wide, a mix of fear and desire in their green depths. "Yes, I'm sure."

I smile, but it's not a nice smile. It's the smile of a man who's about to lose control, to give in to his most primal instincts. Sliding the knife down her body, I trace the path I plan to follow with my tongue. She whimpers, her body shaking, but she doesn't pull away. She wants this, the darker side of pleasure, and I'm going to give it to her.

Pressing just hard enough to break the skin, I draw a thin line of red between her breasts. She gasps, hands flying to the spot, but I hold them at her side and lean down to lick the small cut.

"Delicious," I groan with my face between her tits. "Does me cutting you turn you on?"

She bites the inside of her cheek. "I don't know."

"Liar," I growl, lifting her onto the edge of the table and pulling her legs apart roughly. "Your cunt is fucking soaked. Ready for my cock, isn't it?"

She trembles as she meets my gaze and nods.

"Good girl," I groan, rubbing the head of my cock between her soaking-wet folds. "Time for me to take what's mine."

All hell breaks loose at that moment. Any control I had snapped. I press into her, not gently or slowly. She's tight, so fucking tight, and the feel of her around my cock sends a jolt of pleasure through me. I groan, my hands gripping her hips as I wait a moment, my dick all the way inside her. She claws at me as I stretch her around my size. And then I pull my cock almost all the way out, glancing down to see her virgin blood on my dick.

"Fuck, look at your blood on my dick," I groan, the tip still inside her. "Look at it, baby girl," I demand.

She complies, her eyes widening. Her blood is smeared on my cock, while her legs remain wrapped around my waist. She looks fucking wrecked, her hair wild, her cheeks flushed, and her eyes glassy with desire. It's a picture that will forever be burned into my memory.

I slam back into her, and she makes a strangled sound. "Look at my cock buried deep inside you," I growl. "See how beautiful you are, stretched around me, drenched in your innocence."

Her hands touch me gently, and I perceive the wonder in her eyes. "You're so deep, Aksel. It's—"

"It's fucking perfect," I finish for her, my voice rough with emotion. "You're perfect, wrapped around me like this."

And it hits me, like a punch to the gut, that this girl will be my ruin. This woman, with her wide eyes, inquisitive nature, defiant spirit, and innocent body, has gotten under my skin in a way no one has ever done.

I'm completely and utterly fucked, but I wouldn't have it any other way.

Moving my hips slowly at first, I watch her face as she winces. "I'm going to fuck you now, baby girl. It might hurt a bit, but just relax and take it."

She nods, her eyes closing. I start to thrust slowly at first but soon pick up the pace, my hips slamming into hers.

"Fuck, you feel so good," I grit out, leaning in and claiming her mouth in a bruising kiss. Her taste, the feel of her tongue against mine, drives me to thrust harder, faster, chasing the pleasure that's coiling tight in my gut.

"You like that, baby girl?" I pull back, my breath hot against her neck as I speak. "You like my cock pounding into you, marking you as mine?"

"Yes, fuck," she gasps, her nails digging into my shoulders. "It feels so good. Don't stop."

I chuckle, driving into her. "Wouldn't dream of it, littlefugl. I'm just getting started."

Needing to be even deeper, I wrap an arm around her waist and tilt her pelvis up, hitting a new angle that makes her cry out. "Fuck, Aksel!"

My name on her lips is an aphrodisiac, spurring me harder and faster, driving us toward the edge. I can feel her trembling around me, her body tightening, and I know she's close.

Leaning in, my lips brushing her ear, I murmur, "Come for me, baby girl. Let me feel you fall apart on my cock."

Her hands grip my biceps, her nails digging in as she cries out, her body shaking as she falls over the edge. "Aksel!"

Feeling her clench around me, tightening like a vise, sends me spiraling into my own release. "Fuck!"

Driving into her one last time, I bury myself as deep as I

can go, spilling myself inside her as my name falls from her lips.

Collapsing against her, I feel her arms wrap around me, holding me close. We're both breathing heavily, our sweat-soaked skin slick against each other, and I know there's no going back. This little bird is mine, and I'm hers, whether we like it or not.

13

ZARA

The ache between my thighs is incessant when I wake the next morning, making me groan. A warmth cocoons me as I shift, and I notice the heavy, muscled arm around my waist.

I tense as the memories of last night flood my mind. Aksel's powerful hands roam my body, his intense gaze piercing me, the way he claimed me repeatedly. I can't believe how much I craved his touch, how I begged for more even as he pushed me to my limits.

Thank God I'm on the pill for my acne, or I'd be scared I might have got pregnant last night how many times Aksel came inside me.

My heart races as I feel his warm breath on my neck. His grip on me is firm and possessive as if he's afraid I'll try to flee. The thought of escaping doesn't cross my mind, though. Instead, I find myself melting into his embrace, savoring the heat of his skin against mine.

I shift slightly, and he stirs, his muscles rippling. "Good

morning, littlefugl," he murmurs, his voice thick with sleep. He nuzzles my hair, and I shiver at the intimacy of the gesture.

"Morning," I manage, my voice barely above a whisper.

Aksel's hand slides down my side, sending tingles through my body. "How are you feeling?" he asks.

I swallow hard, unsure how to respond. I'm still reeling from the events of last night, the way Aksel had so thoroughly dominated me and taken my virginity. But I've awoken to his raw power and magnetism, craving more.

"I'm...I'm okay," I finally manage, wincing at how unconvincing I sound.

Aksel chuckles, the rumble of it vibrating against my back. "That's good to hear." His grip tightens, and I know I'm not going anywhere, even if I want to.

I take a shaky breath, my mind racing. "Aksel, I'm not sure what this means, what we mean."

"It means you're mine. My little bird." He kisses the nape of my neck, sending a shiver down my spine. "And I plan to keep you that way."

I swallow hard. "But what about my research? I can't just—"

"Shh." Aksel cuts me off, his thumb caressing my hip soothingly. "We'll figure that out. Right now, you're exactly where you're supposed to be."

I want to protest and insist I have a life and responsibilities outside this cabin. Outside of Noway. I live in Minnesota, for fuck's sake. I turn over to look at him, and the way Aksel looks at me, with a hunger that makes my breath catch, silences any objections.

"I'm not going to let you go," he murmurs. "You belong to me now."

I shudder at his words, partially thrilled at the idea of belonging to this powerful man. The rational scientist in me knows it's impossible. But as Aksel's lips find mine in a searing kiss, all coherent thought flies out the window.

When we finally part, both of us are breathless. Aksel smiles at me, his eyes dark with desire. "Get dressed. I have something to show you."

I nod mutely, my mind reeling while I watch him rise from the bed. As he pulls on a pair of jeans, I can't help but admire how the fabric clings to his thighs, the ink of his tattoos stark against his skin.

Aksel catches me staring and grins. "Like what you see, littlefugl?"

I blush, suddenly self-conscious. "I, um, I..." My voice trails off as Aksel approaches the bed, his movements fluid and graceful.

He leans down, his face mere inches from mine. "Don't worry, baby girl. You'll be seeing a lot more of me from now on."

I swallow hard as he leaves the bedroom and jumps out of bed. Grabbing a sweater and jeans, I get dressed while my mind is on a whirlwind of conflicting emotions: desire, fear, and confusion.

Making my way to the kitchen, I find him leaning against the counter with a steaming mug of coffee in hand. His gaze instantly locks onto me.

"There you are, littlefugl," he rumbles, setting his mug down. "I was starting to think you'd flown away on me."

I shake my head mutely, unable to find my voice momentarily.

Aksel crosses the room in a few long strides, crowding my space until I can smell the earthy scent of his skin and the hint of coffee on his breath. "Come with me," he murmurs, taking my hand. I shiver at his touch but allow him to lead me out of the kitchen.

We stop before the door he took me through last night, and Aksel pauses, looking at me. "Do you like hunting, Zara?"

I blink, surprised by the question. "Um, no, not really," I admit. "I don't like the idea of shooting animals or hurting them."

Aksel's lips turn into a slight smirk, but something is unsettling in his gaze. "Is that so? We'll have to see about changing your mind on that."

Before I can respond, he's opening the door and ushering me inside. My eyes widen as I take in the room we'd been in last night, but I was so wrapped up in him that I hadn't noticed that it's like a hunter's den. The walls are lined with mounted animal heads, weapons, and many creepy-looking masks. This is where we fucked last night, but it was dark, and I hadn't gotten a chance to really look around, too consumed by the man before me.

The mounted animal heads and weapons make me uneasy, but I force a smile onto my face. "Wow, you must really like hunting, huh?" I say, trying to keep my tone light.

Aksel's eyes glint with amusement as he watches me.

"You could say that," he replies, his voice a low rumble. "Hunting is in my blood. It's a way of life here."

I nod, pretending to be fascinated as my nerves kick up a gear. "That's interesting! I've never really been around hunting before."

Aksel steps closer to me, his presence overwhelming in the small space. "Perhaps I could teach you sometime," he murmurs, reaching out to tuck a strand of hair behind my ear. His touch sends a shiver down my spine. "There's nothing quite like the thrill of the hunt, the rush of adrenaline when you have your prey in your sights."

I swallow hard, ignoring how my body reacts to his proximity. "That sounds intense," I manage, my voice wavering.

Aksel chuckles a deep, rich sound that reverberates through my very bones. "Oh, it is, littlefugl. But I think you might enjoy it more than you realize."

I force another smile, determined to keep the mood light. "Maybe! I'm always up for trying new things."

Aksel's gaze darkens, and I realize the double meaning in my words too late. "Is that so?" he murmurs, his hand sliding down to the small of my back. "I'll have to keep that in mind."

I blush, mentally kicking myself for my poor choice of words. "I just meant, you know, like hobbies and stuff," I stammer, trying to backtrack.

But he pulls me closer, his other hand cupping my cheek. "I know exactly what you meant, baby girl," he whispers hotly against my ear. "And I fully intend to explore all the new things we can try together."

I tense as Aksel's grip on me tightens, his body radiating an intensity that sets me on edge. "Why did you bring me in here?" I ask.

Aksel regards me with a serious expression, his brow furrowed. "There's something I need to admit to you."

A knot of dread forms in the pit of my stomach at his grave tone. I swallow hard. "O-Okay..."

He takes a deep breath. "When I first agreed for you to come stay here for your research, I had other intentions for you."

I frown, not liking where this is going. "What do you mean?"

Aksel's gaze bores into me, unflinching. "I had planned to lure you out into the wilderness under the pretense of helping with your work. And then hunt you."

The words hit me like a physical blow, making me recoil from him, sickened. "You were going to hunt me? Like an animal?"

He nods. "That was my original plan, yes. To track you through the woods and eventually..." He doesn't finish the sentence, but the implication is clear.

Bile rises in my throat as the horror of his admission sinks in. Shoving at him, I put some distance between us. This whole time, I had been blinded by my attraction to him. I convinced myself that despite his intensity, he was a good person. But now I see the truth—Aksel is a predator of the worst kind.

"You're depraved," I whisper, my voice shaking. "You were going to kill me?"

Aksel holds up a hand. "I know how it sounds. But

when I met you in person, everything changed. You captivated me in a way I never could have anticipated." His eyes roam over me with undisguised hunger. "You're too special to harm, littlefugl. Don't you see? This is better."

I shake my head vehemently, backing away from him until I hit the wall. "No, this isn't better! You're completely unhinged!"

In that moment, every interaction we've had over the past few days takes on a sinister new light. How this man watched me with such intensity, the subtle threats laced into his words—it all makes sense now. He had truly intended to hunt me like prey.

14

AKSEL

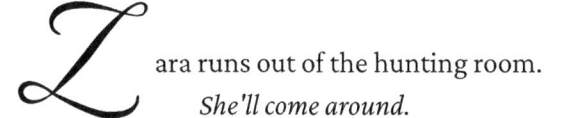

Zara runs out of the hunting room.

She'll come around.

Sure, I intended to kill her before I met her, but the moment I met her, that changed. I can't shake the feeling of disappointment as Zara slams the door, locking herself away from me. I want to break the door down and force her to understand, but that would only reinforce her fear.

Instead, I lean against the door, resting my forehead on the cool wood. "Little bird," I call out. "Don't be scared. I would never truly hurt you."

There's no response, but I can hear her shaky breathing on the other side. I close my eyes, picturing her trembling form, her beautiful face contorted with terror. The thought of her fearing me cuts deep despite my usual indifference to others' emotions.

"I know I said some unsettling things," I admit. "But I live a different life out here, guided by primal instincts, not the rules of society. When I first brought you here, yes, I intended to hunt you like the prey you are."

I pause, running a hand through my hair. "But then I saw you. Really saw you. And everything changed. You awoke something in me, little bird. A hunger, a need that goes far beyond the physical."

Pressing my palm flat against the door, I imagine her on the other side, listening intently. "From the moment I looked at you, I knew you were meant to be mine. And I yours."

There's a slight creaking from inside as if she's moved closer. Encouraged, I continue in a low rumble. "I don't expect you to understand it right now. But I promise you, in time, you'll embrace the truth of who you are. And we'll be unstoppable together."

The silence that follows is heavy and loaded with tension. I can picture her internal struggle, the war between her ingrained sense of right and wrong and the dark, primal urges I've awakened within her.

Just as I'm about to try a different approach, her soft voice filters through the door. "I...I need some time," she says, her tone wavering. "This is all too much, too fast."

A slow smile spreads as I nod, even though she can't see it. "Of course, little bird. Take all the time you need."

Stepping back, I shoot one last glance at the door before turning to leave. *She'll come around eventually.*

After that intense conversation, I head out to the garage, needing space to clear my head. As I step inside, the familiar smells of motor oil and grease provide a strange comfort. This is my realm, where I'm in control.

Grabbing a wrench, I pop my truck's hood and get to work. The repetitive motion of tinkering with the engine quietens my mind for a few blessed moments. But it doesn't last. Zara's face keeps flashing in my mind's eye, those emerald eyes wide with fear and confusion.

I yank harder on a stubborn bolt. What I wouldn't give to have her here with me now, to chase away that haunted look with the heat of our bodies moving together. Just the thought of her soft curves pressed against me is enough to rekindle the fire burning low in my gut.

Gritting my teeth, I try to focus on the task at hand, but Zara has burrowed herself under my skin in a maddening way. It's insane how much I want her and crave her despite having had her multiple times last night. Each encounter only whets my appetite for more.

I recall her first time in the hunting room, how she bled on my dick. The way she trembled beneath me like a frightened doe. The way her innocence shattered with each thrust, those breathy whimpers of pain and pleasure driving me wild. And in the aftermath, cradling her spent body against mine, I knew I could never let her go.

Zara is mine. No matter how hard she fights, I'll never release her from my grasp.

The wrench clatters as I brace my hands on the fender, hanging my head. Get a grip, I chide myself. She'll come around. Once she accepts the truth of what we are, of this primitive bond between us, she'll never want to leave.

Nodding to myself, I straighten and grab a rag to wipe the grease from my hands. There's work to be done. Chores to complete, supplies to gather.

I imagine her by my side, a perfect partner in every sense of the word. Me the hunter and her the prey, only when I catch her I don't hurt her, I fucking breed her like she's meant to be bred.

Yes, that's exactly how it will be. She just needs a little more time to come to realize it.

A soft voice pierces through the air. "Aksel?"

I turn to face her and take in her red eyes and tear-stained cheeks. "Hey," I murmur, irritated that I care that she's been crying. "Are you okay?"

She hugs her arms around herself. "Have you hunted people here before?"

The question hangs heavy in the air between us. The obvious answer is yes—many times. But something stops the admission from passing my lips.

Instead, I meet her watery gaze steadily. "Does it matter?" My voice is a low rumble. "What matters is that I'm done with that life. You've awoken something new in me, little bird."

I step toward her, satisfaction flickering as she holds her ground. "Something primal. Animalistic." Another step, and I'm looming over her petite frame. "You've released the beast inside me, which hungers for you."

Her chest rises and falls with rapid breaths as my calloused fingers trace the delicate line of her jaw. "I want to hunt you, Zara." My thumb brushes her trembling lower lip. "But with a fundamental difference."

She holds her breath, waiting for me to continue.

"I want to breed you because you're my mate. And

whenever I catch you, I'll fuck you as such, fill you with my seed." I press my lips to her neck and bite softly.

A whimper escapes her, eyes fluttering closed at my touch. Good, she's already falling under my spell again. Leaning in, I brush my lips against the sensitive skin below her ear. "Say you're mine, little bird. Say it, and I'll never let you go."

Zara shudders violently in my embrace. "I'm y-yours, Aksel. Yours."

I crush her body against mine, lips claiming her mouth in a searing kiss. She melts into me, all resistance evaporating under my onslaught of passion.

Breaking away, I grip her chin roughly to hold her unfocused gaze. "That's right, you belong to me now. Mind, body, and soul." I punctuate each word with a punishing kiss. "And I'm never letting you go."

She nods shakily, pupils blown wide with desire.

Good girl.

Scooping her up effortlessly, I carry my prize back into the cabin and to my bedroom. Zara clings to me, raining hot, open-mouthed kisses along my neck and jaw in a desperate bid for more.

I'll give her more, alright. By the time I'm through with her, she'll be utterly and permanently ruined for anyone else. Zara is mine to possess, to dominate, to breed.

Kicking open the bedroom door, I deposit her on the bed in a tangle of sheets. She gazes at me lustfully, and something primitive in me roars in approval.

"Get undressed, but leave the shoes," I growl, shredding my clothes. "I want you naked and waiting for me, little bird."

Zara doesn't hesitate, urgently stripping off her clothes with trembling hands as I stalk toward the bed. When she's bare before me, I pounce...

15

ZARA

I've lost the plot. As Axel bites at my skin, devouring me like a hungry animal, I realize how fucked up this all is.

He's killed people. He intended to murder me before we met.

And somehow, I still desire him. How is that possible?

I hesitate, my heart racing as Aksel's intense gaze pierces through me. His large, calloused hands grip my arms, pulling me close.

"Get out of your head, little bird," he demands. "I would never hurt you. Only make you feel exquisite pleasure for the rest of your life."

I shudder at his words, a mix of fear and unwanted desire coursing through me. He pauses, his eyes searching mine.

"Do you want to play with me, Zara?" he asks, his voice low and seductive. "Hunter and prey?"

Part of me wants to run and get as far away from this

dangerous man as possible. But another part that craves his touch, his domination, is intrigued.

"I..." My voice trails off as I struggle to find the words.

He lifts me off the bed, my body bare and exposed, and carries me into the hunting room. It still gives me the creeps.

"I'm not sure about this..." I start, my voice trembling.

He silences me with a fierce look, setting me down on the floor. My legs feel unsteady as he turns to the wall, selecting a mask and a knife. My breath catches in my throat.

"We'll play hunter and prey," he declares, his eyes gleaming. "You'll run, and I'll chase. When I catch you..." His gaze travels down my body, and I shiver. "We will mate."

I swallow hard, my mind racing. Part of me wants to flee this madness and return to the normalcy of home, but another part craves Aksel's touch as if it's the oxygen I need to breathe.

"Okay," I whisper.

A predatory gleam ignites in his gray-blue eyes. "Good girl." He puts on the mask, and suddenly, it feels like the air shifts—as if I'm no longer in the room with the same man.

"Run, little bird," Aksel growls, his voice muffled by the mask. "The hunt has begun."

I take a deep breath, then turn and dart away through the cabin, my shoes slapping against the wooden floor. Adrenaline surges through me as I flee, the hunting room fading behind me.

I burst out of the cabin door, the cool air hitting my

bare skin like a slap, but I barely register it because of the adrenaline coursing through my veins. The dark forest engulfs me as I dash away from the cabin.

My feet pound against the damp earth, twigs and rocks threatening to trip me. The trees loom over me, their shadows stretching long and ominous in the dim light filtering through the canopy.

I can sense Aksel behind me, stalking me like the predator he is. The crunch of his boots against the forest floor makes me shudder.

I veer off the path, my heart hammering in my chest as I weave between the trees. Branches whip at my face, leaving stinging scratches, but I don't slow. I can't let him catch me.

The anticipation builds, a heady mixture of fear and arousal. I risk a glance over my shoulder and immediately regret it. Aksel is closer than I thought, his powerful form cutting through the trees like a force of nature. The mask conceals his face, rendering him a faceless, unstoppable pursuer.

A root catches my foot, and I stumble, gasping as I throw out my hands to break my fall. The damp leaves and soil stick my palms as I scramble back to my feet, my chest heaving.

Aksel's boots appear in my peripheral vision, and I whirl, backpedaling away from him. He advances slowly, deliberately, the knife gleaming in his hand.

"You can't outrun me," he growls, his voice muffled by the mask.

I back away until my shoulders hit the rough bark of a

tree trunk. Trapped. Aksel closes the distance between us, the mask mere inches from my face.

"It's over," he murmurs, and then his hands are on me, consuming me with searing, possessive touches.

His eyes are wild and hungry, peering at me through the holes in his mask as he grabs my hips and drags me into a nearby clearing. I stumble, falling onto my back, and before I can catch my breath, he's on top of me, his body aligning with mine.

There's no gentleness in his touch, only raw, animalistic need. He enters me in one swift thrust, filling me so completely that I gasp. Then he begins to move, his hips snapping as he drives into me over and over.

It's savage and primal, nothing like our first time. There's no tenderness at all. This is pure, unrestrained passion.

I arch my back, matching his rhythm, my hands digging into his muscular shoulders. The sensation is intense and overwhelming. I can feel him everywhere, claiming me and marking me as his own.

The world narrows to the feeling of him moving within me, the sound of our harsh breathing and grunts of pleasure filling the forest. I'm dimly aware of the rough ground beneath me and the cool air on my skin, but all I register is him.

His pace quickens, his breath coming in short, sharp bursts. I sense his control slipping, the raw power of his body taking over as he gives in to his most primal urges.

Our gazes lock, his eyes burning into mine. I can see the desire, the possession, the need to claim me shining in their depths. He surges into me even harder, his hips slamming against mine with enough force to hurt.

His fingers dig into my hips with bruising pressure, but I crave it, needing this primitive connection with him. I wrap my legs around his waist, urging him on, my nails digging into his skin.

"You're mine," he groans, his voice rough with desire. "Mine to mark. Mine to breed."

His words send a shockwave through me, and I realize I want this—all of this. I want him to brand me as his, to leave his mark on my body and soul. As insane as it sounds I want to have his children, to create life with this wild, intense man.

A cry tears from my lips while the pleasure builds, my body tightening around him. Aksel swears, his control snapping as his thrusts become erratic, his body bowing as he pushes me deeper into the earth.

"Little bird, I'm—" he grunts, his eyes clenched shut.

He doesn't need to finish the sentence. I know he's falling, and I'm right there with him, hurtling toward the edge.

Our cries echo through the forest, a chorus of primal satisfaction as we find our release together. Aksel collapses onto me, his breath hot against my neck, sending shivers down my spine.

I hold him tightly, my arms and legs still wrapped around him, never wanting to let go. He lifts the mask and tears it off his face, pressing kisses along my shoulder while his cock remains solid and twitching deep inside me.

"You're mine now," he whispers, his voice husky and filled with possession. "My little bird, my mate."

I turn my head, and we kiss slowly, passionately.

Breathing heavily, Aksel shifts his weight, rolling to lie beside me on the forest floor. He pulls me close, his arm wrapping protectively around me, and together, we stare up at the canopy, where the branches sway gently in the breeze.

"Zara," Aksel murmurs, his voice soft and full of wonder, "I—"

But whatever he's about to say is cut off by a rustling sound nearby. We freeze, our gazes snapping toward the source of the noise. My heart pounds in my chest as I spot movement in the underbrush.

There's another predator in these woods, and it's closing in.

Could it be the wolf?

The rustling in the underbrush grows louder. Aksel tenses beside me, his arm tightening around my waist protectively.

"Stay still," he orders.

I hold my breath, straining to make out the source of the noise. Is it an animal? Or something far more sinister? After what Aksel revealed about his twisted intentions, I can't be sure of anything anymore.

Leaves crunch underfoot, the sound drawing nearer. Aksel shifts beside me, his muscles coiled and ready to strike like a predator sensing its prey. I can feel the adrenaline thrumming through his veins, mirroring my rising panic.

A figure emerges from the bushes. I nearly choke on my relieved exhale when I recognize Tor, the rugged outdoorsman who sat beside me on the flight from the States. His brow furrows as he takes in our entwined, naked forms on the forest floor.

"Well, well," Tor drawls, a knowing smirk tugging at the corners of his mouth. "Seems you two have been getting better acquainted."

Heat floods my cheeks as I scramble to cover myself, clutching fistfuls of leaves and dirt to my chest. Aksel doesn't move, his gaze locked on Tor with violent fury.

"We didn't expect company," Aksel says coolly, not a hint of embarrassment in his tone. His hand trails lazily along the curve of my hip, and I swallow hard, suddenly very aware of my nakedness.

Tor's eyes track the movement, his smirk widening. "So I see. Though I must admit, this isn't quite the scientific research I had in mind when you mentioned it, Zara."

My cheeks burn hotter at his implication. I open my mouth to respond, to defend myself, but Aksel beats me to it.

"How the fuck do you know her name?" Aksel demands.

I clear my throat. "He was sat next to me on the plane. How do you know him?" I ask, glancing between the two men.

"Tor is my cousin," Aksel rumbles. "What do you want, Tor?"

I stare at Tor in disbelief, my cheeks burning with embarrassment at being caught in such a compromising position. What are the odds of me sitting beside Aksel's cousin on the way here? And Aksel never mentioned he had family living nearby.

Tor smirks. "Didn't Aksel tell you? I live a few miles from here at my own cabin." He raises a brow. "Maybe you should visit sometime if this is the kind of treatment you give your hosts."

Aksel growls and scrambles to his feet, not caring that he's completely naked. "Careful cousin."

The smirk on his face makes my skin crawl. There's something predatory in how he looks at us, and I'd have preferred the wolf stumbling on us. I pull the leaves tighter against my chest, suddenly feeling more exposed than ever.

"What are you doing in my territory, Tor?" Aksel's voice is low in warning.

Tor raises his hands in a placating gesture. "Easy there, cuz. I was just out for a hike to come and visit my cousin, enjoying the fresh air." His gaze drifts back to me, and I feel my face flush anew. "Didn't mean to interrupt your activities."

A twisted sort of thrill seems to dance in his eyes.

"Well, you did interrupt," Aksel growls. "Now fuck off."

But Tor doesn't move. He simply stands there, watching us with that infuriating smirk. The silence stretches, thick and heavy, until finally he speaks again.

"You know, when Zara told me on the plane that she was coming here for research, I'll admit, this isn't quite what I pictured."

I open my mouth, but no sound comes out. What could I say to that?

Aksel starts toward him, and I can feel the tension radiating off him in waves. "I won't tell you again, Tor. Get the fuck out of here."

For a long moment, Tor doesn't move. Then, finally, he shrugs.

"Suit yourself," he says easily. "I'll leave you two researchers to it."

With one last lingering look, he turns and disappears back into the bushes, the crunch of leaves and snap of branches marking his retreat.

I release the breath I've been holding, my body sagging with relief. Aksel doesn't relax, though. He stays standing before me, tense.

"He'll be back," Aksel mutters, turning to face me. "We should go. It's not safe out here anymore."

As much as I hate to admit it, he's right. I don't want to be around whatever twisted game Tor is playing when he decides to make his next move.

So I nod and allow Aksel to pull me to my feet. He takes my hand, walking me back toward the cabin briskly.

I can't help but glance over my shoulder as we go, half-expecting Tor to reappear from the tree line. But the forest remains silent, almost mockingly, as if it's holding its breath in anticipation.

And I can't shake the feeling that this is far from over.

16

ZARA

The shrill ring of my cell phone cuts through the quiet cabin, making me jump. I fumble for it on the coffee table, my heart racing as I glance toward the bathroom door. Aksel is still in the shower, the sound of running water barely audible over the pounding in my ears.

I swallow hard as I see the caller ID. It's my boss at the research lab back in Minnesota. Guilt twists my gut as I accept the call.

"Hi, David," I say, trying to keep my voice even and professional.

"Zara! How's the research trip going so far?" His tone is light, but I can detect the slightest hint of impatience.

I glance toward the bathroom again, picturing Aksel's naked form behind that thin door.

"Well, the storm when I first arrived really set me back," I say carefully. It's not a lie, but it's far from the whole truth. "I just got a chance to set up my equipment and take some initial readings a few days ago."

There's a pause on the other end of the line, and I can hear the impatience in David's voice when he speaks again. "I see. And when can we expect your first report?"

My free hand clenches into a fist in my lap. "I'll try to have something for you by the end of the week. But the internet connection here is spotty, so I may have trouble uploading it immediately."

Another pause, longer this time. When David responds, his tone has taken on a distinctly disapproving edge. "You know how important this research is, Zara. I expected more from you."

The words sting, and I bite my cheek to avoid snapping at him. He has no idea what I've been through these past few days. No idea of the mind-bending, life-altering things I've experienced.

"I understand," I say, keeping my voice casual. "I'll do my best to get you that report as soon as possible."

There's a heavy sigh on the other end. "Fine. Just don't let me down, okay?"

The line goes dead before I can respond. I slowly lower the phone, staring at it in my hand as a mix of shame and defiance swirls inside me.

Don't let me down.

The words echo in my mind, and I can't help but let out a bitter laugh. If only David knew the half of it. If only he had any idea what I've already let myself in for here.

The bathroom door opens with a creak, and I look up to see Aksel emerging, a towel slung low around his hips. His skin is still glistening with water droplets, and my mouth goes dry at the sight of his chiseled torso.

He raises an eyebrow at me, clearly having heard my laugh. "Something funny, littlefugl?"

I open my mouth but can't find the words because nothing about this situation suddenly seems remotely funny anymore. "It was my boss from the research lab back in Minnesota."

His eyebrow arches and I feel a shiver run through me at the silent challenge in his expression. As if he's daring me to explain myself further.

I let out a shaky breath. "He wanted an update on my progress here. An initial report on the data I've collected so far."

Aksel's towel rides low on his hips as he moves closer, each step slow and deliberate. "And what did you tell him, littlefugl?"

There's an undercurrent to his words that makes my pulse quicken. A clear implication is that anything less than complete honesty won't be tolerated.

"I...I told him the storm when I first arrived set me back," I admit, unable to meet his eyes. "That I only just started getting readings a few days ago."

Aksel is standing over me now, near enough that I can smell his skin's clean, soapy scent. His hand grabs my chin, forcing me to look up at him.

"But that's not the full story, baby girl?" His voice is a low rumble, sending a shiver down my spine. "You left out the best parts."

My cheeks flush hot with shame and arousal. He's

right, of course. I didn't speak to David about the twisted games Aksel and I have played. The depraved, delicious acts he's introduced me to. The way he's utterly possessed me, body and soul.

"I couldn't tell him that," I whisper, my voice trembling. "He'd never understand."

His grip tightens fractionally, his steel blue eyes holding me in their thrall. "Of course he wouldn't," he murmurs. "He couldn't imagine that the sweet and innocent scientist he hired has been thoroughly ruined by me."

His words send a molten spike of need lancing through me. Because it's true—Aksel has ruined me, stripped away every last shred of the prim and proper woman I once was, and remade me into something raw and wanton and ravenous for his touch.

I don't know whether to be ashamed or proud of that fact. All I know is that the fire he's stoked inside me burns hotter and brighter with every passing moment.

"No, and he won't understand if I don't work through the night to get this report done for him."

Aksel grabs my wrist as I reach for my laptop, and a thrill of apprehension runs through me. His eyes blaze with an intensity that makes my breath catch.

"You don't need to worry about that report anymore, littlefugl," he rumbles, his voice a deep, gravelly purr. "You're not going to be returning to Minnesota."

I can only gape at him in stunned silence for a long moment. Not returning? But my job, research, and entire life are back there. How can he possibly think I'd abandon all of that?

His free hand cups my cheek as if reading my mind, brushing his calloused thumb over my lips. "I know what you're thinking, baby girl. You're wondering how I can ask you to give up everything you've worked for."

His gaze bores into me, equal parts commanding and seductive. "But you must understand—you've awakened something primal inside me since I first saw you. An insatiable hunger to claim you as my own, to make you mine in every possible way."

A shudder ripples through me at his words' low, velvety rasp. I should be outraged, disgusted at his arrogant presumption that I'd give everything up for him. But instead, I find myself leaning into his touch like a sunflower turning toward the sun, utterly entranced.

"From the moment I tasted your sweet innocence, I knew you were meant to be my mate," he continues, his thumb tracing the curve of my lower lip. "And a beast like me doesn't let his mate slip away."

His words conjure a vivid image—Aksel as a great predator in the wilderness and me as the hapless little bird caught in his sights.

"But my work..." I try to protest, even as my body arches shamelessly into his touch. "I can't abandon everything I've worked so hard for."

Aksel's laugh is low and dark, like the rumble of distant thunder. "Can't you, littlefugl?" His fingers tangle in my hair, gripping firmly enough to make me gasp. "After everything we've shared, you'd still choose that sterile little lab over the wildness I can offer you?"

His lips brush against my earlobe. "I've ruined you for

anything less than the freedom of the hunt, baby girl. You and I know there's no going back to that caged existence you had before."

A whimper escapes my lips as desire crashes over me in dizzying waves. Because damn him, he's right—the woman I was before is gone, sloughed off like a shed snakeskin. In her place is someone rawer and feral, who craves the untamed world Aksel introduced her to.

As if sensing my surrender, Aksel's grip on my hair softens to a sensual caress. "That's my good girl," he purrs, dragging his lips against my jaw. "Don't fight what you know to be true, littlefugl. You belong to me now, in the life I can give you. No more cages, no more constraints, just the thrill of the hunt and the pleasure of being mine."

His mouth claims mine in a scorching kiss, and I melt against him, all resistance gone. Because he's right—I'm his now, in mind, body, and spirit. And as terrifying as that reality is, I know there's no escaping the wildness he's awoken in my soul.

"What am I going to do about work, though?" I breathe, shaking my head. "My boss won't be happy, and I've got all the equipment—"

"Don't worry about that, baby girl," he rumbles. "I'll make sure your boss gets the message, loud and clear."

Then his mouth crashes down on mine, swallowing my gasp of surprise as he kisses me deeply, possessively. And in that endless, searing moment, I know there's no going back.

Not that I'd ever want to.

17

AKSEL

Glancing out the window, I scan the surrounding forest for signs of life. Tor is a threat. All our lives, he's been trying to one-up me. Seeing me with Zara, I know he'll want to take her from me.

Tor has spent his life living similarly to me. He'll see Zara as a prize free for the taking, and I can't have that. If I have to kill him, then so be it.

Zara emerges from the bedroom, rubbing the sleep from her eyes. "What are you doing?" she asks.

I turn to face her, not wanting to reveal the messed-up thoughts racing through my mind. "Just scoping out the area," I say nonchalantly, forcing a casual shrug.

She regards me momentarily, those piercing green eyes seeming to bore into my soul. I tense, wondering if she can sense the darkness lurking within.

But then she clears her throat. "We should invite Tor over for a meal this evening."

The idea makes my jaw clench. The last thing I want is

that smug bastard near Zara or my territory. "I'm not sure that's a good idea, baby girl," I say, trying to keep my tone even.

Zara frowns, crossing her arms over her chest. The motion makes the thin fabric of her shirt strain against her full breasts, and I have to tear my gaze away to focus. "Why not? He's your family."

"Exactly." I rake a hand through my hair, thinking of an excuse she'll accept. "Things can be complicated with family. Especially Tor. You don't want to get caught in the middle of that."

Her brow furrows. "Is everything okay between you two?"

I smile reassuringly, stepping closer to run my knuckles along her soft cheek. "Everything's fine. I just prefer to keep certain parts of my life separate, that's all."

Zara worries her full lower lip between her teeth, a gesture that makes my cock stir. But after a moment, she gives a small nod. "Alright, if you're sure."

Relieved, I pull her against me, breathing in her intoxicating scent. "I'm sure. Now, how about I make us some breakfast?"

Zara's eyes light up at the mention of breakfast. "That sounds amazing," she says with a bright smile like a ray of sunshine piercing through the darkness I surround myself with.

As I turn toward the kitchen, my mind is whirring, calculating my next move. Tor can't be allowed to interfere in this.

She leans back against the counter, watching me. "So

tell me about your family. I'd love to hear more about where you come from."

The request makes me tense, the easygoing domesticity we'd been enjoying evaporating instantly. I don't like talking about my past or the people in it. Most of them are dead anyway—either at my own hand or because the world is an ugly, unforgiving place.

Keeping my back to her, I focus on cracking eggs into a bowl, trying to keep my voice casual. "Not much to tell, really."

"No siblings? How many aunts and uncles?" she presses, ever inquisitive. Doesn't she know some things are better left buried?

A wave of darkness washes over me as memories of my parents' cruelty resurface—things I've tried so hard to bury.

"My parents were harsh," I say finally, keeping my back to her as I crack eggs into a bowl more forcefully than necessary. "Survival of the fittest was their philosophy. They raised me to be a hunter, to take what I wanted by any means."

I can still hear my father's gruff voice, berating me for any show of weakness.

"You're the alpha, boy. Ain't no room for softness if you want to make it in this world."

Zara must sense the tension radiating off me because she doesn't push further. A heavy silence stretches between us as I continue mechanically prepping our breakfast.

Finally, she speaks again. "Is that why you and Tor

don't get along? Some sort of alpha rivalry between you two?"

A harsh bark of laughter escapes my lips at the irony. If only she knew the full truth—that my father had drilled that toxic alpha mentality into us from birth, insisting there could only be one in a family.

My father used to make me watch from a young age when he mated with my mother and my aunt, his sister. As well as other women in the family. Since she lived with us, and he was the alpha male, he was the one who had to satisfy and breed any women living with us. Tor and I are actually half-brothers as well as cousins, but Tor is inbred, and it fucked with him a bit mentally. He's far more unhinged than me.

"Something like that," I mutter, jaw clenching at the memories. I can still hear the cold, emotionless tone in my father's voice the day he gave me the choice—kill or be killed.

A tremor runs through me as I remember the shock of realizing my own father expected me to take his life. Still, the will to survive had been ingrained in me so deeply that, in the end, I did what I had to.

I clear my throat, eager to shift the conversation away from the darkness of my past. "Enough about me and my family. Tell me about yours. What were your parents like growing up?" There's a part of me that is shocked to even hear me ask.

Zara gives a small shrug. "Oh, you know, pretty typical, I guess. My dad was a high school football coach, and my mom was a homemaker."

A wistful look crosses her delicate features. "They've always supported me and my interests, even when I decided to go into atmospheric science instead of something more traditional for a small-town Minnesota girl."

I nod along, genuinely interested in learning more about the woman who has so thoroughly captivated me. "You were a small-town girl? I can't quite picture that."

A low, melodious laugh escapes her lips. "Why? Because I'm too sophisticated and worldly for you?"

"Something like that," I tease. "Though I definitely wouldn't call you sophisticated."

Zara gasps in mock offense, swatting my arm playfully. "Hey, watch it! This small-town girl will put you in your place."

"Is that a promise?" I growl, pulling her flush against me so she can feel the effect her playful banter is having. Her breath catches, those green eyes darkening with desire.

Clearing her throat, she tries to regain her composure. "As I was saying, yes, just a typical Midwestern upbringing. We didn't have much, but my parents made sure my brother and I never wanted for anything."

The mention of a sibling piques my interest. "You have a brother?"

She nods. "Mmhmm, Kyle. He's a few years older than me. Followed in our dad's footsteps and now coaches at our old high school since dad retired a couple years ago."

I keep my expression neutral, but I can't stop the jealousy that courses through me at the thought of another man in her life—even if he is just family. The irrational part of my brain doesn't care about the details. All it knows is the white-hot possessiveness I feel over her.

"Sounds like you were close with your brother growing up," I say carefully, watching her face for any telling reaction.

Zara's eyes soften. "We were. Typical sibling stuff—we fought like cats and dogs sometimes, but I could always count on Kyle having my back when it mattered." A wistful smile tugs at the corners of her mouth. "I remember this one time in middle school there was this bully who kept tormenting me about my braces. Kyle found out, and the next day at school, he...well, let's just say that kid never messed with me again after that."

My jaw clenches at the thought of some little punk harassing what's mine. The urge to track this person down and make them pay is overwhelming. She seems to pick up on the tension rolling off me in waves.

"Aksel? Are you okay?" She places a gentle hand on my arm, brow furrowed with concern.

Forcing myself to unclench my fists, I give her what I hope is a reassuring smile. "Yeah, sorry. Just got a little heated there thinking about someone treating you like that."

Zara moves a little closer. "It's okay," she murmurs, trailing her fingers up my arm, raising goosebumps in their wake. "That was a long time ago, and Kyle ensured I was protected, just like you do now."

The implication of her words isn't lost on me. She sees me as the new protector in her life, someone who will go to violent lengths to keep her safe if needed.

Pulling her against me, I kiss her with feral desperation. Zara melts into me with a soft moan, her nails scratching lightly at the nape of my neck and sending shockwaves of pleasure down my spine.

When we finally break apart, both of us are panting harshly. Zara's lips are swollen from my assault, her eyes glazed over with pure want. I stare at Zara silently, trying to process my emotions. Emotions I didn't even know I was capable of feeling.

My entire life, I've been taught that showing vulnerability or softness is a death sentence. Yet here I am, utterly disarmed by this beautiful woman and her genuine care for me.

As I gaze into Zara's warm green eyes, something deep within me stirs to life. A part of me I thought was long dead—beaten down by years of my father's cruel "survival of the fittest" mentality.

I was raised to be a ruthless hunter. To take what I wanted without remorse or hesitation. Emotions like empathy or tenderness were viewed as weaknesses to be purged.

But Zara awakens something primal yet oddly gentle inside me. An aching need to protect her, to keep her safe in a way that has nothing to do with possessing her as my prize.

My chest tightens as flashes of my childhood assault my mind. My father's incessant derision and scathing putdowns whenever I dared show an ounce of compassion.

"You want to end up a sniveling little bitch, boy? Emotions like that'll get you killed."

I can still hear the biting tone in his gravelly voice and see the disgust etched into the hard lines of his face. It was as if he was ashamed to even acknowledge that I was his son.

No wonder I turned out this way—a cold, callous killer without an ounce of remorse. Emotions were systematically trained out of me from an early age and replaced by an insatiable hunger to hunt and dominate.

Yet here I am now, trembling on the edge of something. Some vast, terrifying new realm of feelings that part of me craves to explore, even as the rational part screams to shut it all down.

Is this what love feels like? The irrepressible urge to protect and cherish someone, to put their needs before your own? If so, it's no wonder my father always treated it with contempt.

Because love, I'm realizing, is the greatest weakness of all. It makes me vulnerable in a way that goes against every core instinct I have as a hunter.

Zara senses the internal war raging inside me. Her delicate brows knit together in concern as she cups my face tenderly.

"Aksel? What's wrong?" she murmurs, running her thumb soothingly along my cheekbone.

I open my mouth but shut it again. How can I possibly explain the torrent of emotions battering against the icy walls I've spent a lifetime constructing?

Instead, I do the only thing that makes sense. I crush my lips to hers in a searing, desperate kiss.

Pouring every ounce of the rawness and vulnerability

into our scorching embrace, seeking solace in the soft curves of her body and the intoxicating vanilla scent of her hair.

This frightening new path I find myself hurtling down is one I cannot turn back from. Not anymore.

Because whether I'm ready or not, Zara has awoken the fragile heart I never knew I had. A heart I thought was ripped out and buried long ago. And I'll be damned if I let anyone—including my own inner demons—take that from me now.

18

ZARA

The tension radiates off Aksel as he remains silent, refusing to answer my question about what's troubling him. Darkness lurks beneath his stoic exterior, a hidden pain I desperately want to understand and soothe. But instead of opening up, he sweeps me into his arms, lifting me effortlessly as if I weighed nothing.

Aksel carries me into the bedroom, his piercing gaze never leaving mine. He lays me gently on the bed, his large frame looming over me, making me feel small and delicate in comparison.

Aksel's rough, calloused hands begin to explore my body with a reverence that steals my breath away. His touch is electric, igniting a fire threatening to consume me whole. He lavishes me with attention, his lips trailing scorching kisses along my neck, collarbone, and cleavage.

I arch into his touch, craving more, needing to feel his skin against mine. He strips me slowly, deliberately, his eyes drinking in every inch of my exposed flesh like a man starved. When I'm finally bare before him, he steps back, his gaze raking over me possessively.

"You're mine, Zara," he growls, his voice low and rough with desire. "I won't let anyone take you from me."

I shiver at his words, at the raw possessiveness in his tone.

Aksel strips and joins me on the bed, his powerful body covering mine, his weight pressing me into the mattress.

His mouth crashes down on mine, hard and demanding. His hands are everywhere, tugging at my hair, gripping my hips, branding me with his touch. I can feel the ridge of his arousal against my thigh, and I moan, rubbing myself against him mindlessly.

"That's it, baby girl. You want me, don't you?" His voice is thick and strained with need.

I nod frantically, unable to speak as he teases and nips at my neck. His teeth scrape my sensitive skin, and I cry out, my fingers digging into his broad shoulders. He tastes and marks me, his beard scratching my skin.

"Say it," he grunts, his hands tightening on my hips as he grinds against me. "Tell me what you want."

My cheeks flame with heat, but the words spill from my lips, driven by the insistent throbbing between my legs. "I want you. I want your cock. Please give it to me."

His eyes darken at my plea, the pupils expanding. His mouth crushes mine again as he pushes inside me, filling me with one swift stroke. We groan at the intimate connection, the heat and pressure building between us.

Aksel moves, his hips snapping as he thrusts into me with primal need. The force of his thrusts rocks the bed while he grabs my thighs, pulling me tighter against him. My legs wrap around his waist, meeting his rhythm and rising to greet each powerful stroke, our bodies moving in harmony.

His hands roam, cupping my breasts, squeezing and kneading. His thumbs tease my nipples. "Do you like it when I fuck your sweet little cunt?" He teases my nipples with his thumbs. "You love it when I touch, mark, and breed you."

I can only whimper in response, lost in the pleasure. Aksel's words are dirty, but they ignite a fire in my core that has me clawing at his back. "More," I gasp.

He bends his head, capturing a nipple between his teeth and biting down gently. "You're mine," he growls. "I'm going to mark you with my mouth, my cock. Everyone will know you're taken."

Aksel's relentless rhythm pushes me closer to the edge, and my body tightens, my breath quickening as pleasure coils low in my belly. His hands squeeze my ass, pulling me tighter against him, and he accelerates, his hips slamming into mine.

"That's it, baby girl, come for me. Let me hear you scream." His breath is hot against my ear, his voice a low, guttural growl.

His words push me over the edge, and my body convulses, waves of pleasure rippling through me. I cry out, my back arching off the bed.

"That's my good girl," he grunts, his thrusts becoming more erratic as he chases his own release. "Your tight little cunt is milking my cock."

The filthy words fuel the fire burning between my legs. I want more of his dirty talk and possession.

Aksel's pace becomes frenzied as he loses control, his hips snapping wildly as he surges toward his climax. His hands grip my hips, his fingers digging into my flesh as he growls my name. "Zara, fuck, you're so tight. I'm gonna—"

He groans, his body stiffening as he empties his cum inside me, his release triggering a second wave of pleasure that has me crying out again, my body shaking with the force of my orgasm.

We lie tangled together, our hearts pounding, breathing raggedly. I feel his lips press against my forehead, his hand stroking my hair. A sense of contentment washes over me, an overwhelming feeling of satisfaction.

But as I lie there, his words echo in my mind.

You're mine, Zara... I'm going to mark you... everyone will know you're taken.

A shiver runs down my spine, and I realize with a start that he's not just marking my body—he's marking my soul.

I understand there's no going back. I've surrendered myself to this man, body and soul. Whatever happens next, whatever darkness lies in store, I know I'm his forever.

But then, a new realization hits me. The knowledge that I belong to him doesn't scare me the way it should. In fact, an unfamiliar sense of peace washes over me. It's as if I've finally found where I belong—in the arms of a man who's as beautiful as he is broken.

A man named Aksel.

19

ZARA

I step outside the cabin, grateful for the brief reprieve from the relentless rain. The crisp mountain air fills my lungs as I set up my equipment, preparing to take atmospheric readings. It's been a week since our tense encounter with Tor, Aksel's cousin, and the unease still lingers.

Aksel was adamant that Tor would try to interfere, but there's been no sign of him so far. I can't help but wonder if his paranoia is justified or simply a manifestation of his possessive nature.

As I calibrate the sensors, my mind drifts to the tumultuous emotions I've been grappling with since that fateful night when Aksel first fucked me.

Aksel's gravitational pull draws me deeper into his world. Yet, a part of me still yearns for the safety and familiarity of my old life, the one I left behind in Minnesota.

The data begins to stream in, and I lose myself in the

familiar rhythm of recording and analyzing. It's a welcome distraction from the chaos that has become my reality. It reminds me of the woman I once was before my host awakened these fierce longings within me.

Footsteps behind me break my concentration, and I turn to find him approaching, his piercing gaze fixed on me. A shiver runs down my spine as he draws near, his proximity igniting a fire within me.

"Taking readings?" he asks, his voice a low rumble that sends tremors through my body.

I nod. "The conditions are ideal."

Aksel steps closer, his fingers grazing my arm, leaving a trail of goosebumps in their wake. "Perhaps we should take advantage of the weather," he suggests.

I know what he's implying, and a familiar ache blossoms between my thighs.

"I really need to get more data to send to my boss before he fires my ass." I turn back to my equipment.

Aksel's fingers trail along my arm, sending shivers down my spine. I try to focus on my work, but his presence is overwhelming, consuming my every thought.

"You may as well get fired," he says. "You're never going back to America."

His words hit me like a freight train, and I spun around to face him, my heart pounding. "What?" I ask, even though I know he thinks I'm staying here.

Aksel steps closer, his body pressing against mine. I can feel the heat radiating off him, the raw power emanating from his every pore. "You belong to me now, little bird," he murmurs, his breath hot against my ear. This is your home, here with me."

I swallow hard, my mind reeling. Part of me wants to resist, assert my independence, and cling to the life I once knew. But another part of me, the part that has been awakened by this rough man, yearns to surrender to him completely.

"I can't just abandon everything," I protest, even as my body melts into his embrace.

Aksel's hand cups my cheek, tilting my face to meet his gaze. His eyes are intense, burning with a possessive desire that takes my breath away. "You already have," he says softly. "The moment you stepped into my world, you left your old life behind."

I know he's right. The pull between us is too strong, too primal to resist. I've been caught in his web, ensnared by the raw masculinity that pours off him in waves.

"What about my research?" I ask, a final, feeble attempt at resistance.

Aksel's lips curve into a smirk. "You'll have all the data you need right here," he promises, his hand sliding down my back, pulling me flush against him. "Set up your own blog or whatever shit people do nowadays. Be independent in your research."

Aksel's suggestion lingers in my mind, the possibility of conducting my research independently, free from the constraints of a traditional academic setting. The idea is thrilling and terrifying, a leap into the unknown that could propel my career to new heights or send it crashing down in flames.

I chew on my bottom lip, weighing the pros and cons. On one hand, the freedom to pursue my passions without the constant pressure of deadlines and bureaucratic red tape is incredibly appealing. I could delve into the areas of study that truly fascinate me without having to justify my every move to my boss.

But on the other hand, the thought of striking out on my own is daunting. Without the backing of a respected institution, would my work still be taken seriously? Can I get the necessary equipment to conduct my experiments?

As if sensing my hesitation, Aksel pulls me closer, his strong arms enveloping me in a cocoon of warmth and safety. "You're brilliant, Zara," he murmurs, his lips brushing against my temple. "You don't need anyone else to validate your work. You have everything you need right here, with me."

His words are like a balm to my soul, soothing my doubts. In Aksel's eyes, I see a reflection of the woman I could be; confident, independent, and unafraid to chase my dreams.

"You really think I could do it?" I ask.

Aksel's fingers tilt my chin, forcing me to meet his gaze. "I know you can," he says with unwavering conviction. "You're a force of nature, Zara. Nothing can stand in your way."

His faith in me is a heady rush that courses through my veins like wildfire. Aksel is more than just a lover or a protector—he's my anchor. The one person who truly sees me for who I am and believes in my potential.

The idea of forging my path with Aksel suddenly doesn't seem so daunting anymore. It feels like the beginning of a new chapter of a thrilling adventure that I'm ready to embark on.

20

AKSEL

Watching Zara across the table, the fireplace's warm glow illuminates her delicate features. She takes a bite of the steak, a hint of a smile playing on her lips as the flavors dance on her tongue. A sense of contentment washes over me, and I am captivated by the simple pleasure of sharing a meal with her.

"This is delicious, Aksel," she says, her green eyes sparkling with appreciation.

I nod, savoring the moment. "I'm glad you enjoy it, littlefugl."

Zara blushes at the affectionate nickname.

We chat about her research, and I listen intently as she explains the intricacies of atmospheric patterns. Her passion for her work is infectious, and I find myself drawn deeper into her world with every word she speaks.

Suddenly, a deafening gunshot pierces the tranquil silence, shattering one of the cabin's windows. Glass rains down around us, and Zara screams, instinctively ducking for cover.

I immediately know it's Tor, the bastard trying to lure me out. Without hesitation, I grab Zara and pull her close, shielding her from potential danger.

"Stay low," I growl, scanning the broken window for movement.

Zara clings to me, her body trembling. The need to get her to safety overwhelms me. Keeping her head down with my hand, I guide her toward the hunting room, the only part of the cabin without windows. I slam the door shut as we enter, locking it behind us.

"Aksel, what's happening?" Zara whispers.

I pull her close, my hands gripping her shoulders firmly. "It's Tor," I growl, anger coursing through my veins. "He's trying to force my hand."

Zara's brow furrows and I can see the questions forming in her mind. But there's no time for explanations, not when she's at risk.

"Listen to me," I demand. "You're going to stay in here until I've dealt with him. No matter what you hear, you stay put. Do you understand?"

I gaze into Zara's eyes, seeing the fear and confusion swirling within. She deserves to know the truth, but revealing the sordid details of my past could shatter the fragile connection we've formed.

"Tor and I..." I begin, struggling to find the words. "Our relationship is complicated, to say the least."

Zara's brow furrows, her lips parting as if to ask a question. But I hold up a hand, silencing her.

"There's a lot about my childhood and upbringing that you don't know," I say. "Things that would make even the strongest recoil in horror."

I can see the curiosity burning in her eyes, but I shake my head firmly.

"Now is not the time for such revelations," I growl. "All that matters is keeping you safe from Tor's twisted games."

A loud thud echoes from outside, and Zara flinches, instinctively pressing closer to me. I wrap my arms around her, pulling her against my chest, savoring the warmth of her body.

"Trust me, little bird," I murmur, my lips grazing her ear. "No matter what happens, I won't let any harm come to you."

Zara nods, her body trembling as another crash resonates through the cabin. I tighten my embrace, determined to shield her from the darkness that has haunted me for far too long.

I release Zara from my embrace and turn toward the wall lined with hunting gear. My fingers trace the cold metal of the knives and rifles, tools I've become intimately familiar with over the years. This is my domain, where I reign supreme as the hunter.

"Promise me you'll stay here," I command, pressing my lips over hers. "Under no circumstances do you leave this room, understood?"

She nods in response.

I quickly don my hunting attire, the familiar weight of the garments a comforting presence. As I strap on my boots, I glimpse Zara huddled in the corner, her arms wrapped around her knees. The sight of her vulnerability tugs at something deep within me. Lastly, I grab my rifle and a hunting knife from the wall.

"Lock the door behind me, baby girl," I breathe, glancing one more time in her direction before stepping back into the cabin. The air is tense, the silence broken only by the occasional thud from outside.

As I approach the front door, I pause, listening intently for any sign of Tor's whereabouts. The bastard is cunning; I'll give him that, but he underestimates the lengths I'll go to protect what's mine.

With a deep breath, I fling open the door and step out into the cool night air. The forest surrounds me, a vast expanse of shadows and potential dangers. But I'm no stranger to this realm. This is my territory, and Tor has just become my prey.

I move silently through the trees, my senses heightened, every fiber of my being attuned to the slightest sound or movement. Tor is out there, somewhere, waiting to strike. But he doesn't know the depths of my determination, the primal fury that courses through my veins.

This is a reckoning long overdue, a settling of scores that should have happened years ago. Tor's actions have sealed his fate, and I won't rest until I've dealt with him.

As I venture deeper into the forest, the shadows close around me, but I remain undeterred. I will emerge victorious, no matter the cost. The alternative doesn't bear thinking about.

The shadows dance in the pale moonlight filtering through the canopy above. My senses are heightened, every nerve ending alive and alert as I scan the vicinity for signs of Tor.

There! A fresh set of footprints, the indentations in the damp earth leading deeper into the woods. A feral grin tugs at my lips as I recognize Tor's heavy tread. The fool thinks he can outmaneuver me on my own territory.

I follow the trail, my steps silent and measured, the weight of the rifle in my hands a comforting presence.

But then, something catches my eye—another set of footprints leading in the opposite direction toward the cabin. My heart skips a beat as realization dawns on me. Tor's game has turned sinister, and Zara is the sole target.

A primal roar tears from my throat as I whirl around, abandoning Tor's trail and sprinting toward Zara. The trees blur past me, but my focus is unwavering. A single thought consumes my mind: protect my little bird at all costs.

As the cabin comes into view, a scream shatters the silence, a sound that chills my blood and sets every nerve ending ablaze. It's Zara's scream, and it's filled with terror.

I redouble my pace, my lungs burning with exertion, but I push forward, fueled by a fury that knows no bounds. The cabin door looms ahead, and I brace myself for the worst, steeling my resolve for whatever horrors await within.

21

ZARA

I cower in the corner of the hunting room, my heart pounding relentlessly against my ribs. The silence is deafening, each passing second amplifying the dread coiling in my stomach. Where is Aksel? What's happening out there? A thousand terrifying scenarios race through my mind, each more unsettling than the last.

Suddenly, a thunderous crash shatters the stillness, causing me to scream in terror. The door leading outside explodes inward, shards of wood scattering across the floor. Through the haze of debris, a menacing figure emerges—Tor clad in hunting gear, his face contorted into a sinister smirk.

"Well, well, what do we have here?" He drawls.

I feel utterly exposed, like helpless prey trapped in the sights of a skilled hunter. But it's completely different from how Aksel looks at me. It's filled with pure malice. And I know in that moment that Aksel was telling the truth, ever since we met he never intended to hurt me, even if it was his initial motivation for inviting me here. "Aksel's little plaything," he sneers, stepping closer. "I must admit, I didn't expect him to grow so attached."

My heart thunders in my ears as Tor advances, his movements calculated. I press myself further into the corner, desperate to distance myself as much as possible.

"You see, Zara," Tor continues, his tone dripping with condescension, "Aksel and I have a complicated history. We're more than just cousins—we're brothers, bound by blood and a legacy darker than you could ever imagine."

A shiver runs down my spine at his words, and I can't help but wonder what secrets lie beneath the surface of Aksel's mysterious past. How can Tor be his brother and cousin?

Tor pauses, his eyes glinting with malice. "And now, it seems my dear brother has developed a fondness for you." He chuckles. "But don't worry. I'll take good care of you, just like Aksel would."

I cower against the wall, Tor's imposing frame towering over me. His words chill me to the bone.

"You see, Zara," he drawls, his voice dripping with menace, "Aksel and I were raised to believe there could only be one alpha male in the family. The strongest and most dominant survives." His lips curl into a sinister smirk as he rakes his gaze over my trembling form. "And now that he's claimed you as his mate, it seems I have no choice but to take you for myself."

My heart drops into my stomach as the full weight of his words sinks in. He wants to mate with me? A wave of nausea washes over me.

Tor's smirk widens, his eyes glinting with a predatory gleam. "Don't look so frightened, little bird," he purrs, using Aksel's nickname for me in a mocking tone. "I promise I'll be gentle at first."

Before I can react, he lunges forward, his powerful hands clamping around my wrists like vises. A strangled cry tears from my throat, and I thrash in his grip as he pins me against the wall. His body presses against mine, trapping me, suffocating me with his overwhelming presence.

"Get off me!" I scream, panic clawing at my throat. "Aksel! Help!"

Tor merely chuckles, his hot breath fanning across my face. "Your precious Aksel can't save you now," he sneers. "You're mine."

His free hand snakes around my waist, pulling me flush against him. I can feel the hard planes of his body through the layers of clothing separating us, and bile rises in my throat. This can't be happening. This has to be a nightmare.

"Please," I sob, tears streaming down my cheeks. "Please, don't do this."

But Tor is relentless, his grip tightening as he leans in closer, his lips brushing against the shell of my ear. "Struggle all you want," he growls. "It'll only make this more fun for me."

My heart races, terror gripping me in its icy clutches. A thunderous roar echoes through the room when I'm convinced all hope is lost.

Aksel storms in, his eyes wild and feral, like a beast unleashed from its cage. In an instant, he takes in the scene before him. Tor trapping me, his hands roaming my body. A guttural snarl rips from Aksel's throat, raw and primal, sending chills down my spine.

"Get your filthy hands off her!" he growls.

Tor merely smirks, his grip on me tightening. "Or what, brother? You'll have to kill me to stop me from claiming what's rightfully mine."

In a blur of motion, Aksel lunges forward, his powerful frame slamming into Tor with the force of a raging bull. They crash to the ground, a tangle of limbs and fury, snarling and grunting like feral animals locked in a battle for dominance.

I shrink back against the wall, my body trembling as I watch the brutal scene unfold before me. Fists fly, connecting with sickening thuds as the two men grapple and claw at each other. It's a primal display of raw power and violence, a side of Aksel I've briefly witnessed when he came up against the wolf.

Tor gains the upper hand, pinning Aksel to the floor and raining down a flurry of blows. But Aksel is relentless, his rage fueling his strength. With a surge of adrenaline, he bucks Tor off, reversing their positions and unleashing a barrage of punches.

The air is thick with the metallic scent of blood, the grunts and snarls of the two men echoing off the walls. I can't look away from the savage display, my heart pounding in my throat as I watch the man I thought I knew transform into a beast.

Aksel's movements are fluid and lethal, each strike precise. He's a force of nature, a whirlwind of fury driven by an instinct so primal that it borders on terrifying. And yet, even as I witness this raw, untamed side of him, I can't help but feel a twisted sense of awe.

Tor struggles beneath Aksel's onslaught, his defiance slowly waning as blow after blow rains down upon him. Finally, with one last devastating punch, Aksel punches Tor to the floor in a bloody heap. And I'm sure, as I look for any signs of breathing, that Aksel has killed him.

22

AKSEL

The acrid scent of blood hangs thick in the air. Adrenaline courses through my veins while I stand over Tor's motionless form, his blood pooling around his body. My knuckles throb from the force of our violent clash, a grim reminder of the depths I've sunk to protect what's mine. Father got his wish after all—there can only be one alpha male.

A movement in my peripheral vision catches my attention. I whirl around to see Zara backing away toward the door.

I swiftly move to block Zara's path, my primal instincts taking over as I grab her arm. She lets out a gasp, her eyes widening in fear.

"Let me go!" she cries, struggling in my firm grasp.

Immediately, I loosen my hold, though I don't release her completely.

"Zara, wait," I rasp, my voice still ragged from the fight. "You don't understand."

"You killed him!" she accuses, glancing over at Tor's lifeless form. "Your own brother!"

I swallow hard. "Half-brother," I correct her quietly.

She looks at me in horror and disbelief.

"I had no choice," I say urgently. "It was either Tor or me. That's the way it's always been."

I can see the questions swirling in her eyes. She deserves to know the truth, no matter how dark and twisted.

"There are things you need to understand about my past, about my family," I tell her. "Things I've tried to leave behind, to erase from my memories."

I release her arm and rake a hand through my hair.

"My father was a monster," I continue. "The kind of evil that leaves deep scars passed on through blood. He pitted Tor and me against each other from birth, determined to breed only the strongest alpha male."

Zara shakes her head, struggling to comprehend.

"We were just boys," I say bitterly. "But in my father's eyes, we were animals. Creatures meant to fight and dominate."

I meet her gaze steadily. "Tor gave me no choice tonight. It was self-defense, kill or be killed. That's the legacy my father left us."

Zara looks down, processing my words. I can't begin to imagine what must be running through her mind.

"I'm not asking you to forgive or forget what you witnessed here," I tell her. "Only to try and understand that this blood feud wasn't of my making."

I reach out and tilt her chin up gently so she meets my eyes again.

"Since the day I left home, I've tried to forge my own path, separate from my father's twisted legacy," I say fervently. "Meeting you, knowing you, has only strengthened my resolve to leave that darkness behind for good."

Zara searches my face as if gauging the truth of my words.

"I know you're scared and confused right now," I say gently. But I give you my word: I'll never intentionally harm you."

I pause, letting my promise sink in.

"Will you at least let me try to explain?" I ask. "To help you understand the demons of my past?"

Zara hesitates, conflicting emotions playing across her delicate features. Finally, she gives a small, tentative nod. Relief washes over me. This is my chance to break the chains of my past, to step into the light with her by my side.

I step closer. The darkness that has shaped my very existence hangs over me. But as I gaze into Zara's eyes, I know this is the reckoning moment. The time has come to lay bare the secrets that have haunted me for far too long.

"My father was an animal, a savage ruled by primal desires," I begin, my voice low. "From the moment I was old enough to understand, I saw how he used his role as the alpha to take whatever woman he wanted."

I pause, old memories threatening to overwhelm me. Zara watches me intently, her body tense.

"He would force himself on the women under our roof

in front of me and Tor from a young age. At every turn, he would exert his dominance. My mother, my aunts—no one was safe from his depravity."

I run a hand over my face, shame creeping through me.

"When my aunt, his sister, became pregnant with Tor, I felt a sick relief that the child was male. Had Tor been born a girl..." I trail off, bile rising in my throat at the thought of my father fucking a possible sister before me.

Zara's eyes widen in understanding, her skin paling.

"My father ruled our household like his personal harem. The women were conditioned to obey his every command, no matter how vile. The boys were taught in his image."

I meet Zara's gaze, seeing my anguish reflected in her eyes.

"Tor and I share the same cursed blood, bound by the sins of our father. But I vowed long ago to break that cycle, to claw my way out of the darkness that shaped me."

My hands curl into fists at my sides. Zara's eyes are wide, her lips parted in anticipation as she awaits the darkest truth of my existence.

"When I came of age, my father summoned me," I begin, my voice hoarse. "He looked at me with those cold, dead eyes and said there could only be one alpha."

I swallow hard, the memories threatening to overwhelm me.

"It was a battle to the death. Kill or be killed. Much like this one with Tor today. That was the only way to assume the mantle of leadership in our twisted household."

Zara's hand flies to her mouth, stifling a gasp. I can see

the horror in her eyes, but I press on, needing her to understand."

I fought with everything I had, driven by a primal instinct to survive. In the end, I emerged victorious, my father's lifeless body at my feet." I pause, the weight of that moment still bearing down on me, even years later.

"But the true test was yet to come," I continue. "My mother, aunts, and the other women all looked at me with expectation."

Zara's brow furrows.

"They wanted me to assume my father's role, take them as my mates, and breed them like animals."

The words leave a bitter taste in my mouth, but I force them out, needing Zara to understand the full scope of the darkness I've escaped.

"The thought of continuing that cycle of depravity sickened me to my core. I couldn't bring myself to become the monster my father was."

I take a shuddering breath, the memories threatening to overwhelm me.

"So I left. I turned my back on that twisted household. I vowed never to return, never to perpetuate the cycle of abuse and subjugation. However, I did take with me a dark blood lust that I struggled to satiate."

My gaze meets Zara's, and I see the tears glistening in her eyes.

"That's the truth, Zara. The ugly, twisted truth of my past. I know it's hard to comprehend, but I needed you to understand the depths of darkness I've escaped but not been untouched by."

I reach out, my fingers brushing her cheek gently.

"You're the only reason I've ever had to fight against the shadows that threaten to consume me. And I promise you, I'll never let that darkness touch you, no matter what it takes."

Zara cups my face gently, her touch sending a shockwave of tenderness through me. Her eyes, those emerald pools of light, shimmer with unshed tears as she gazes up at me.

"I'm so sorry, Aksel," she whispers, her voice thick with emotion. "No one should have to endure the darkness you faced as a child."

Her words are laced with empathy and understanding, piercing through the walls I've erected around my heart. "You've been through hell," Zara continues, her thumb tracing the sharp line of my cheekbone. "No wonder you're consumed by darkness after witnessing such depravity."

I swallow hard, my throat constricting with emotions I've suppressed for far too long.

"You don't have to apologize," I rasp, my voice hoarse with the weight of my past. "The sins of my father are not yours to bear."

Zara shakes her head, her golden tresses swaying with the movement. "But I can help shoulder the burden. Let me be your light, your beacon in the darkness."

I gaze into her eyes, searching for any hint of fear or revulsion, but find only warmth and acceptance.

Before I can speak, Zara rises onto her tiptoes, her warm, curvy body pressing against mine. Her lips find mine in a searing kiss, a desperate embrace that speaks of her unwavering devotion.

I respond with fervor, my arms encircling her, pulling her closer. Our kiss deepens, a passionate dance of tongues and shared breaths, a merging of souls transcending the physical.

The hunt is over. Her scent, a heady mix of vanilla and roses with an underlying musk, fills my nostrils as I stand over her. My breath comes in ragged gasps, my heart pounding with primal desire. She's mine now, the spoils of war.

With a growl, I tear at her clothes, exposing her creamy skin. Her eyes follow my every move. I can't wait any longer.

Hoisting her up, I lay her back on the hunting bench, her skin marred by smears of my blood. She looks wild and beautiful, her blonde hair tumbling around her head like a halo.

I shed my clothes, leaving me bare and hard, my cock straining with need. I position myself between her thighs, eager to claim what's rightfully mine.

"You're so fucking beautiful," I rasp, my voice thick with desire. "My victory prize."

I stroke her inner thigh with my thumb, a smile curving my lips as she shivers in response.

"Do you know what victors do to their spoils, little bird?" I ask.

She bites her lip, a nervous gesture that only fuels my arousal. "No," she breathes.

"They take what's theirs," I growl, leaning in close so

my breath fans her ear. "And that's exactly what I'm going to do."

I kiss her neck, reveling in the feel of her soft skin against my lips. My hand slides up her thigh, inching higher, teasing her.

"You're so wet for me, baby girl," I murmur, my hand cupping her pussy. "Your tight little cunt is mine now."

She lets out a choked gasp as my fingers slide inside her, stroking and teasing. I smirk at her reaction, loving her responsiveness to my touch.

"That's it, take my fingers," I encourage, my thumb circling her swollen clit. "You're going to come all over my hand, and then I'm going to fuck that pretty pussy raw and breed you so many times that my cum will be spilling out of you."

"Oh God," she moans.

"Don't call out to God, baby. I'm the only power you'll bow to." I bite her shoulder so hard I break the skin and then lap up her blood like a man starving.

Her hands grip my shoulders as I plunge my fingers deeper inside her, her hips thrusting upward to meet my rhythm. My free hand tangles in her hair, tilting her head back to expose the delicate line of her throat.

"I'm the only man you'll ever fucking spread these legs for," I declare, claiming her mouth in a brutal kiss. "Mark my words. By the time I'm done with you, you'll be ruined for anyone else."

Her body bows off the table, her back arching as I bring her to the edge. Her walls clench around my fingers, signaling her release. I growl with satisfaction, feeling her muscles pulsing.

Without warning, I withdraw my hand and position myself at her entrance. The tip of my cock teases her wet heat, both of us savoring the anticipation. She moans, eyes locking on mine. "Please, Aksel."

"Fuck," I breathe, fighting for control. I thrust forward, burying myself to the hilt. "You feel so fucking good with your tight little cunt wrapped around me like this."

Her eyes meet mine as I stretch and fill her. Her nails dig into my shoulders, leaving stinging tracks as I move.

"That's it, little bird," I encourage. "Wrap your legs around me. Take every fucking inch." Her legs lock around my waist, her body rising to meet my savage thrusts. I drive into her, my hips slamming against hers, our flesh slapping together. I growl, pulling out almost completely before snapping my hips forward, burying myself deep. "Tell me you love my cock."

"Yes!" she cries out, her nails raking my back. "I love it!"

Her words make me thrust harder, pounding into her with wild abandon. The hunting room echoes with the sounds of our union, the slap of skin, our labored breathing, and our animalistic grunts.

While we fuck, the shadows of my past recede, eclipsed by the radiant light that is Zara. Her love and acceptance are my salvation, a lifeline pulling me from despair.

With Zara wrapped around my cock, I find solace, a sanctuary from the demons that haunt me.

And in that moment, I know that no matter the challenges, I will never again be alone in the darkness.

23

ZARA

The warm water cascades over me as I stand numbly in the shower, trying to process everything that has happened. I can still feel Aksel's possessive grip on my body, his passionate kisses trailing fire across my skin. My fingers caress the tender spots where his mouth and teeth marked me as his earlier. But my mind keeps flashing back to the bloody violence I witnessed between him and Tor.

I scrub at my arms, desperate to remove the blood he got on me while we fucked. The memory of Tor's dead body haunts me, even though Aksel swore he only killed his brother to protect us. My stomach churns as I recall the sickening thud of flesh striking flesh, the feral rage in his eyes.

The steaming water turns my skin pink, but the thoughts swirling through my mind won't disappear.

Why did Tor call me "little bird" when he burst into the room? How long was he lurking outside, observing us to hear Aksel call me that? A chill runs through me despite the heat of the shower.

Right now, Aksel is digging a hole to bury his brother. It's hard to believe how fucked up his family was. I recall how gentle Aksel was after their brawl, patiently explaining his tortured past.

He claims he has left that toxicity behind, but it's clear it's not entirely true. He invited me here so he could "hunt" me to the death. When he fought with Tor, I saw his love for the fight and the inner demons raging within.

My heart aches, wanting to believe Aksel can conquer that darkness with me by his side. But Tor's attack shattered the illusion of safety in this cabin. I don't know who to trust anymore in this foreign wilderness.

Shutting off the water, I step out and dry myself. Wiping the fog from the glass, I steel myself and assess the constellations of purple and red adorning my neck. Revulsion and arousal war within me, this visible proof of Aksel's claim on me confusing.

Dragging on layers of clothing like armor against my host's magnetic pull, I need space to think. Could I give up everything and continue down this path with him? My research was supposed to be the purpose of this trip.

The sudden ring of my phone makes me jump, my heart racing as I see David's name flash across the screen. Shit. I knew this call was coming, but I'm not prepared to face his wrath after everything that's transpired.

Steadying my trembling fingers, I accept the call. "H-hello?"

"Zara? What the hell is going on?" David's voice booms

through the speaker, dripping with impatience. "I expected your first report days ago. This is completely unacceptable!"

My chest tightens as his accusations pierce me. He can't understand the horror I witnessed in this twisted wilderness only a few hours ago. How can I possibly explain the tangled web of obsession and violence that's ensnared me?

"I...I know, David. There have been some complications," I stammer, my words failing me.

"Complications?" He scoffs. "That's no excuse, Zara. This research is crucial, and you're jeopardizing everything with your lack of professionalism."

White-hot anger flares within me at his callous dismissal. Doesn't he understand that my life has been in danger? That I've been forced to confront the darkest depths of human depravity?

"You've got no idea what I've been through," I snap, my voice trembling with barely contained rage. "I've faced things you couldn't imagine in your worst nightmares."

There's a pause on the other end, and I can almost envision David's stunned expression. But at this moment, I don't care about decorum or propriety. I'm done being the meek, obedient scientist.

"Listen here, you arrogant prick," I seethe, the words tumbling from my lips. "I've been through hell, and you berate me like some incompetent child? Fuck you, David. Fuck this research, and fuck everything else."

His sputtering protests sound on the other end, but I've reached my limit. I end the call with a vicious tap, enjoying the satisfying silence that follows. My hands are shaking, adrenaline coursing through my veins as I struggle to catch my breath.

Free, that's how I feel. Unshackled from the constraints of my former life. Aksel has awakened something primal within me, a ferocity that refuses to be tamed or controlled. I may be his "little bird," but I'm no longer content to remain caged and docile.

I type a quick text to David.

> If it wasn't obvious. I quit.

And then send it to him, my heart hammering at a thousand miles an hour. A newfound freedom washes over me as I gaze out the window at the vast, untamed wilderness surrounding the cabin. This rugged world is my domain now, a place where I can spread my wings and soar without the suffocating expectations of society holding me down.

A slow, satisfied smile tugs at my lips as I toss my phone aside. Whatever challenges lie ahead, I know I'll face them with the same untamed spirit that courses through my veins.

I watch Aksel through the cabin window, his powerful muscles rippling with each thrust of the shovel as he fills the grave. A chill should run down my spine at the sight, but an unexpected sense of pride swells within me.

Tor's lifeless body lies buried beneath that freshly turned earth, a casualty in Aksel's battle to protect what's his. To protect me.

The memory of Tor bursting into the hunting room, his eyes wild with obsession as he declared his intent to claim me, still sends shudders through my body. But Aksel didn't hesitate. He fought with a primal ferocity to defend his territory, his mate.

I was his prize, the object of their brutal conflict. Even as I witnessed the savagery of their clash, I felt no fear of Aksel. His violence wasn't directed at me but was a means to eliminate the threat Tor posed. Aksel's nature was laid bare before me. He is the alpha, the apex predator who'll stop at nothing to safeguard what belongs to him.

And I belong to him, wholly and completely.

The nausea I felt at the sight of Tor's broken body has dissipated, replaced by an overwhelming sense of belonging—of being chosen. Aksel could have let Tor take me and surrendered his claim to avoid bloodshed. But he didn't. He fought for me, risking his life in the process, all to keep me by his side.

As Aksel finishes filling the grave, his gaze lifts, meeting mine through the glass. His eyes lock onto me, blazing with that untamed intensity.

This man, this powerful, dangerous hunter, has claimed me as his mate.

He's my protector, my lover, my everything. And I'm his, forever marked by his passion, strength, and unwavering determination to possess me.

A slow smile curves my lips as I watch him approach the cabin. I may have been the unwitting prey when I first arrived in this wilderness, but now, I embrace my role as Aksel's mate with open arms.

His gaze burns into me as he enters, igniting a fire deep within my core. I move toward him, drawn like a moth to his flame, and without a word, I wrap my arms around his sweat-slicked body, reveling in the scent of earth and musk that clings to his skin.

There is no guilt, no fear, no hesitation. Only the certainty that I am where I belong.

24

AKSEL

Zara speaks with her boss on the phone, her voice laced with frustration. The man's demands for the return of the equipment fill me with irritation. To return the equipment, Zara has to go back to the States.

When Zara hangs up, the weight of her boss's words settles over her. I can see the tension in her shoulders and the uncertainty in her eyes. "He says if I don't return the equipment, he'll come here himself to get the equipment and drag me back to Minnesota," she says, her voice small. He thinks I've lost my mind."

A low rumble escapes my throat. "Let him try," I growl, my fingers clenching into fists. "I'll kill him if he so much as sets foot in my territory."

Zara's eyes widen at my word. "Aksel, you can't be serious," she whispers.

I step closer to her, my gaze unwavering. "I'm deadly

serious, little bird," I say. "No one, and I mean no one, will come here and take you away from me."

She opens her mouth, perhaps to protest, but I silence her with a gentle touch to her cheek.

"You belong to me, Zara," I murmur, my thumb caressing her soft skin. "And I will never let anyone take you from me. If your boss dares to set foot near this cabin, I'll show him the true meaning of survival of the fittest."

The intensity of my words sinks in, and I can see the conflict within her. Part of her is terrified of my violent side, I know, but there's also a spark of something else—a glimmer of understanding, perhaps even a hint of desire.

I pull her close, enveloping her in my embrace, and she doesn't resist. "You're mine, little bird," I whisper, my lips brushing against her ear. "And I'll do whatever it takes to keep you safe."

I pull Zara onto my lap, feeling her soft thighs against my own. Her skirt hikes up, baring her long, slender legs, and I can't resist the urge to slide my hands up, caressing her smooth skin. She lets out a soft gasp, her breath hitching as she feels my cock against her.

"I made you pancakes," I breathe against her neck.

She rocks her hips against me, seeking friction. "Not sure I'll be able to focus on the pancakes," she moans.

With a devilish smirk, I free myself from the constraints of my pants, letting my hardness spring free. I hear her breath quicken and feel her body stiffen momentarily before relaxing against me. I nuzzle her neck, inhaling her sweet scent, and then, with a slow, deliberate motion, I slide inside her.

"Aksel," she murmurs. "What are you doing?"

I chuckle, the sound rumbling in my chest. "Cock-warming, baby girl," I whisper, my lips brushing her ear. "I want you to keep me nice and warm while you eat these pancakes."

Her cheeks flush, a delicate pink spreading across her skin as she realizes my intent. She shifts against me, a slight movement that sends a jolt of pleasure through me.

I pick up a forkful of pancakes and bring it to her lips. She opens her mouth obediently, taking the bite, her eyes never leaving mine. I savor the sight of her full lips wrapped around the fork, the syrup glistening on her lips.

As she swallows, I feel her body relax further against mine.

"Good girl," I murmur, nipping at her skin. "Just like that, little bird. Keep me warm while I take care of you."

I feed my little bird, forkful by forkful, and her eyes glaze over with a mixture of hunger and frustration. She whimpers softly as her hips begin to rock against me, slowly at first, then with growing insistence.

A smug smile spreads across my face. "Seems like you're enjoying breakfast as much as I am, baby girl," I purr, my voice deep and husky.

She lets out a shaky breath, her hips stuttering to a stop. "A-Aksel," she stammers, her cheeks flushed. "I—I can't help it. I want you so badly."

I still her with a firm hand on her hip, my eyes flashing with a warning. "Don't you dare try to milk my cock, little bird," I growl. "You know the deal. You're here to keep my cock warm, not to get greedy."

Her lips part in a silent gasp, her eyes sparkling. She knows better than to disobey me, but the hunger in her eyes betrays her.

"Be a good girl and sit still," I instruct sternly.

Zara bites her lip, her eyes flicking to where we're joined. She swallows hard, her throat working as she suppresses a moan. Her hips twitch ever so slightly, and I feel her inner walls clench around me.

I growl a warning, my hand tightening on her hip possessively. "Don't even think about it, baby girl. Nice and still while I feed you."

She whimpers, her body trembling with the effort of holding still. I can feel her heat, her need, and it only serves to fuel my desire.

"That's it," I murmur, stroking her cheek. "Fight that insatiable fucking lust of yours."

Her hunger for me is palpable, and it only fuels my desire to possess her completely as she squirms even more.

"Easy there, little bird," I murmur, lifting another forkful of pancakes to her lips. "You know the rules. No moving, no greedy little whimpers. Just sit still and let me feed you."

Her eyes flutter closed as she obediently takes the next bite. I can feel her inner walls clenching around me, her body betraying her need.

"That's a good girl," I praise. "Now, why don't you tell me about your family? It might help distract you from that little ache between your thighs."

Zara's eyes snap open, her cheeks flushing with desire

and embarrassment. "M-my family?" she stammers, her voice trembling.

I chuckle, my fingers trailing along her thigh. "Yes, little bird. Your family. The people you left behind to come here and be mine."

She swallows hard, her gaze flickering away from mine for a moment. "Well, there's not much to tell. I told you it was just my parents and my brother. I have aunts and uncles, but we're not particularly close."

I hum thoughtfully, taking another bite and offering it to her.

"And how do you think they'll react when you tell them you're not returning?" I ask. "That you've chosen to stay with me in the wilderness?"

Zara's breath hitches, her eyes widening. I can see the conflict in her gaze, the struggle between her desire for me and the lingering ties to her old life.

"I...I don't know," she murmurs, her voice soft. "They won't understand. They'll think I've lost my mind."

I tut softly, shaking my head. "Now, now, little bird. Don't be so hard on yourself. You haven't lost your mind at all. You've found your true self."

I lean in, my lips brushing against her ear. "You belong here, with me. In the wild, where you can be free and uninhibited. Where you can embrace your primal urges without shame."

Zara shivers, her body trembling against mine. I can feel her arousal growing, her inner walls fluttering around my cock.

"Aksel," she breathes, her voice tinged with desperation. "I...I can't..."

"Shh," I soothe, trailing kisses along her jawline.

Her eyes flutter closed, and a soft whimper escapes her lips.

With a wicked grin, I lean in and capture her lips in a searing kiss, claiming her mouth with a fierce possessiveness. She melts against me, her body pliant and yielding.

Her body betrays her eagerness. I feel her needy little whimpers against my neck as she bucks her hips, seeking the friction she craves. She knows not to disobey, but her hunger for more is plain to see—and feel.

A smile curves my lip. "What's this, baby girl?" I purr, nipping at her lobe. "Can't control that naughty little pussy of yours?"

"P-please, Aksel," she whimpers, her voice shaking. "I need more. I need you to fuck me, please."

I chuckle, the sound deep and rumbling. "You can't keep my cock warm without begging for more, huh?" I tease, giving her a slight rock of my hips to demonstrate exactly what I'm denying her.

"You're such a naughty little slut, aren't you, Zara?" I murmur, twisting my fingers in her hair and forcing her head back roughly. "Couldn't keep that greedy cunt of yours still if your life depended on it."

She moans, her eyes fluttering closed as I tweak her nipple. "Please," she begs, her voice hoarse. "I'm sorry, I can't help it. Just please, fuck me and make me yours."

I smirk, loving having my girl completely at my mercy.

I tighten my grip on her hair, tugging at it to let her know I'm in control.

"Since you asked so nicely, baby girl," I growl, grabbing her hips and lifting her off my cock before slamming her back down. "Take it. Take my cock nice and deep."

A keening whimper escapes her as I fuck her with hard, relentless thrusts. She's breathless, boneless against me, and I know she's hanging on by a thread.

"Good girl," I praise, peppering kisses along her jawline, even as I mercilessly pound into her. "That's how you keep my cock warm, little bird. You take it hard and deep, and you beg for more."

Her climax builds. I can feel it in the flutter of her inner walls, the way she squeezes me like a vise. "Come for me," I murmur, my lips brushing her ear. "But keep those greedy thighs of yours nice and wide. Let me see how wide you can stretch for me."

At my words, she cries out, her body convulsing around me as she shatters into a million pieces. I feel her inner walls pulsing, milking me, and it takes every ounce of my control not to follow her over the edge.

But I'm not done yet. I slow my thrusts, drawing out her pleasure, relishing her soft, satiated whimpers. "That's it, little bird," I croon, kissing her forehead gently. "Ride that high for me. Let your pussy milk my cock."

Zara shudders, her body trembling in the aftermath of her release, and I can feel the slight convulsions of her inner walls as they continue to pulse around me.

"A-Aksel," she breathes.

Her words trail off into a moan as I start to move again, slow and deep, drawing out her post-orgasmic bliss.

"I...I can't—oh God—"

"So sensitive, aren't you, little bird?" I purr, nipping at her neck, marking her as mine. "My greedy little slut, always wanting more."

She whimpers, her fingers digging into my arms, her thighs clenching tight around my hips. "I can't help it," she gasps, her voice pleading. "It's too much, Aksel. I can't—"

I cut off her words with a particularly deep thrust, silencing her with a groan. "Can't what?" I challenge, withdrawing almost completely before thrusting back into her. "Can't take it? Or can't get enough?"

"B-both," she stammers, her eyes squeezed shut as I pound into her. "I can't take any more, but I need—oh, God, Aksel—more!"

I pull out of my little bird's cunt, and with a savage growl, I sweep the plates off the table. Zara gasps, her eyes widening as the porcelain shatters, but she doesn't protest as I bend her over the table. Her skirt hikes up, baring that luscious ass I've been dying to claim.

I can't resist the urge to bite one plump cheek, marking her as mine. She cries out, her body tensing.

Stepping back, I grab a bottle of olive oil and pour a generous amount onto my palms. I smirk as I rub my hands together, feeling the slick liquid warm between my fingers.

"Now," I purr, tracing a finger down the crack of her ass. "It's time to give my little bird something she needs."

She stiffens, her body going rigid. I know this is new

territory for her, and the anticipation is thrilling. Slowly, I pour the oil onto her tight little hole, watching it gleam in the flicker of firelight.

I hear her sharp intake of breath as I tease her, circling my finger around her entrance. "Relax, baby girl," I murmur, my voice low and soothing. "Just breathe. I'll take care of you."

With gentle pressure, I press the tip of my finger against her, slowly pushing inside. She tenses, her body resisting, but then, with a soft gasp, she relaxes, letting me in.

"That's it," I praise, working my finger slowly in and out. "So tight. Just relax and let me open you up."

I scissor my fingers, adding a second, stretching her, preparing her for what's to come. She whimpers, her body trembling, but she nods, urging me.

"Please, Aksel," she breathes, her voice thick with desire. "I need—I need you inside me. I need to feel you in my ass."

I chuckle, the sound dark and dangerous. "As you wish, baby girl," I growl, lining up the head of my cock with her hole. I slowly push against her, feeling her tense around me. I pause, giving her a moment to adjust, before pushing forward, claiming her virgin ass.

A strangled moan escapes her throat as I sink into her, inch by delicious inch. "Fuck," she whispers, her voice hoarse. "It's too much, Aksel. It hurts."

"Shh, baby girl," I soothe, even as I pull back before thrusting forward, claiming her a little more. "It's supposed to. But I promise, the pain will fade, and soon, you'll beg for more."

I slowly stretch her, filling her. She's so fucking tight around me, squeezing me like a vise, and I have to clench my jaw to maintain control.

"That's it," I groan, withdrawing almost completely before slamming back into her. "Take it. Take my cock in that tight little ass."

She's whimpering now, her body trembling with each thrust, but soon, the pain will fade, leaving only pleasure in its wake.

I grab her hips to pull her back onto me. "Take what you need. Milk my cock with that greedy little ass of yours."

I take her hard and rough against the kitchen table, claiming her ass as hers shrieks and pleas echo through the cabin, mingling with the steady patter of rain outside.

Her cries fuel my desire, driving me deeper. I own her now, body and soul, and she knows it. Her nails dig into the table, scratching the wood as she meets my brutal thrusts with abandon.

"Fuck, Aksel," she gasps, her voice hoarse with need. "Harder. I need you harder."

A cruel smile stretches my lips as I grasp her hair, yanking her head back. My cock slams into her again and again. Each thrust a declaration of ownership.

"Beg for it, baby girl," I growl, my breath hot against her ear. "Beg for my cock to ruin that tight little ass of yours."

"Please, Aksel," she whimpers, her body trembling

with each impact. "I need it harder. I need you to fuck me harder."

I chuckle, my grip on her hair tightening as I snap my hips forward, burying myself to the hilt. "As you wish, little bird," I grunt, setting a brutal pace. "Let's see how much you can take."

Her cries fill the cabin with a symphony of pleasure and pain. Her ass clenches around me, begging for more. I give it to her, each thrust harder than the last, driving us both closer to the edge.

"You like it rough, don't you, baby girl?" I snarl, pulling her hair harder, forcing her upper body to arch backward. "You like it when I use that tight little body of yours for my pleasure."

"Yes, Aksel, yes!" she cries, her voice thick with desire. "I'm yours. Take me, claim me, mark me. I'm your dirty little slut."

My cock twitches inside her at her filthy words, and I know I won't last much longer. My lips brush her ear as I whisper, "Come for me, baby girl. I want to feel you shatter around me."

Her body tenses, every muscle corded with anticipation, and then she comes apart with a piercing scream, her ass clenching and releasing around my cock. I feel her pussy squirt, coating my thighs, and it's too much.

With a feral growl, I let myself go, claiming her ass as mine, pumping my release deep inside her. Her hole milks me for every fucking drop, and I know this is only the beginning.

We fall apart, breathless and sated. Zara turns her head

to look at me over her shoulder, her eyes shining with adoration.

"Mine," I growl, leaning forward to claim her lips in a searing kiss while my cock remains deep in her ass. "Now and forever, little bird. You're mine."

She shudders at my possessive words, her eyes fluttering closed as she melts into my embrace. "Yours," she whispers, her lips brushing mine. "Always and forever, Aksel."

25

ZARA

I stare at my phone, my heart pounding as I see Mom flashing on the screen. Taking a deep breath, I brace myself for the barrage of questions. With a shaky hand, I answer the call.

"Zara? Sweetheart, is everything alright?" My mom's voice is laced with worry, and I can picture the crease between her brows as she frets over my well-being.

"I'm fine, Mom," I reassure her, trying to sound calm and collected. "What's going on?"

"David called us," she says. "He said you quit your job and that we need to pay for the equipment you took to Norway."

I close my eyes, angry at David for involving my parents in this mess. "I'm sorry, Mom," I begin, taking a deep breath. "David is overreacting."

"Zara, what's going on? Are you coming home?"

I pause, my mind racing as I consider my options. A

part of me longs to return to the safety and familiarity of my life in Minnesota, but another part yearns to stay in this wild, untamed place with Aksel. His touch, intensity, and raw passion have become a drug that I can't shake.

"Yes, Mom," I finally say, making a decision. "I'll be on tomorrow's flight back home. I need to take care of a few things here first."

"Oh, thank goodness," my mom breathes a sigh of relief. "We were so worried, honey. Your father and I were ready to hop on a plane and come get you ourselves."

I manage a small chuckle, trying to ease her concerns. "That won't be necessary, Mom. I'll be home soon, and we can talk about everything then."

After a few more reassurances and promises to be careful, I hang up the phone and let out a long exhale. My eyes drift toward the window, where I can see Aksel, his powerful strokes easily splitting the logs. Seeing his rippling muscles and how his shirt clings to his sweat-dampened skin sends a bolt of desire through me.

Stepping outside into the pure mountain air, I feel invigorated as I approach him. Aksel pauses, his chest heaving, and turns to face me, a predatory gleam in his eyes.

"Littlefugl," he rumbles, reaching out to tuck a stray strand of hair behind my ear. His touch is electric, and I fight the urge to lean into his embrace.

"Aksel, we need to talk," I begin, my voice steadier than expected. He arches an eyebrow but remains silent, waiting for me to continue.

"I need to go back to Minnesota for a little while," I say, watching his expression carefully. A flicker of anger flashes across his face, but it's gone as quickly as it appeared.

"And why would you need to do that?" he asks, his tone deceptively calm.

I take a deep breath, choosing my words carefully. "I need to return the equipment I borrowed from the lab and explain to my parents that I'm moving to Norway to be with you."

Aksel's eyes widen slightly, and momentarily, I see a glimmer of vulnerability. But then his features harden, and he steps closer, his imposing presence making me feel small and fragile.

"And what makes you think I'll let you leave?" he growls.

I swallow hard but hold his gaze, refusing to back down. "Aksel, I need to do this," I say. "I need to tie up those loose ends so I can be here with you without any distractions or obligations holding me back."

He regards me silently for a long moment, his eyes searching mine. Finally, he lets out a slow exhale and nods. "Very well, littlefugl. But I'll be coming with you."

Relief washes over me, and I can't help but smile. "Of course." I touch his corded arm. "I wouldn't have it any other way."

Aksel pulls me into a searing kiss, his lips claiming mine with a possessive hunger that leaves me breathless. When we finally break apart, his eyes are dark with promise.

"You're mine, Zara Driscoll," he declares. "And after this little trip, there'll be no more distractions or obligations. Just you and me, together in this wilderness, forever."

As we break apart, I gaze at Aksel, my heart pounding with a rush of emotions I can no longer contain. "I love you, Aksel," I whisper, the words tumbling out before I can stop them.

His eyes widen, and for a moment, I fear I've said too much, pushed too far. But then his expression softens, and he pulls me close, enveloping me in his powerful embrace.

"Love is a strange concept for me, littlefugl," he murmurs. "For so long, I've lived in a world of darkness and primal instincts. But what I feel for you..." He trails off, his grip tightening as if afraid I might slip away.

I hold my breath, waiting for him to voice the feelings that have been simmering between us since we met.

"What I feel for you is like a raging fire," he finally says, his words laced with an intensity that sends shivers down my spine. "A fire that burns away the shadows of my past, consuming everything in its path until only the purest of embers remain."

His hand cups my cheek, his thumb tracing the curve of my jaw with a tenderness that belies his rugged exterior. "You're the spark that ignited that flame. The light that guides me through the darkness, leading me toward a future I never dared to imagine."

I lean into his touch, my heart swelling with the weight of his words, the depth of his emotions.

"I may not understand the concept of love as you do,"

he continues, his eyes holding mine captive. "But what I feel for you is a force more powerful than any I've ever known. A bond that transcends mere physical desire or possessive instincts."

He pulls me closer, his lips brushing against my forehead in a feather-light kiss. "You're mine," he whispers, his voice thick with emotion. "And I'm yours, now and forever, bound by a fire that will never be extinguished." He kisses me again, deeply and passionately.

I can't believe how deeply I've fallen for this broken, twisted man, but in his arms, I've found my true home—a place of belonging I never knew existed until I came to this wild Norwegian wilderness.

As our lips part, I gaze up at Aksel, his rugged features softened by emotion. At that moment, I see the man beneath the hunter, the soul scarred by a past so dark and primal that it would break most people.

Yet, despite the shadows that linger in his gaze, there is a warmth there, a tenderness reserved solely for me. My fingers trace the intricate tattoos on his arm.

Aksel's hand covers mine. "These markings tell the story of my lineage," he murmurs, his voice a low rumble that sends shivers down my spine. "A tale of savagery and primal instincts, of a family bound by darkness and twisted traditions."

I hold his gaze, silently urging him to continue, to share the burden of his past.

"But you, littlefugl," he says, his thumb caressing my cheek with a tenderness that belies his rough exterior. "You have rewritten my story, blazing a new path where love and light can flourish, even in the most barren landscapes."

His words resonate deeply, burning away any lingering doubts or fears. Undoubtedly, I belong here, in this rugged wilderness, by Aksel's side.

26

AKSEL

I pace the hotel room, my heart racing faster than ever during a hunt. The thought of meeting Zara's parents makes my palms sweat. I'm not used to interacting with normal people and trying to make a good impression. It's foreign territory, and I feel like a caged animal.

Zara emerges from the bathroom, her blonde hair cascading over her shoulders. She notices my agitation immediately.

"Aksel, what's wrong?" she asks, her green eyes filled with concern.

I run a hand through my hair, struggling to find the words. "I'm... nervous," I admit, the confession strange. "I don't do well with people, Zara. Your parents are going to hate me."

Zara approaches me, her scent of vanilla and roses calming me. She places a hand on my chest, right over my thundering heart.

"They won't hate you," she says softly. "They just want to meet the man I love. You don't have to be anyone but yourself."

I scoff. "Myself? A psychopath with a dark past and blood on his hands? I'm sure that'll go over well with your father."

Zara's eyes harden. "You're more than your past, Aksel. You're the man who protected me, who loves me fiercely. That's who they'll see." She stands on her tiptoes and presses a gentle kiss to my lips. "Besides, I returned David's equipment and left my old life behind. I'm with you now, no matter what. We're in this together."

Her words soothe me somewhat, but the anxiety still gnaws at my insides. I've never cared about anyone's opinion, but I'm desperate for her parents' approval.

I fidget with my tie for the hundredth time, cursing. The damn thing feels like it's choking me, a constant reminder of how out of place I am in this polished hotel.

Zara notices my discomfort and gently touches my arm. "Aksel, take it off," she says. "There's nothing wrong with just wearing a shirt. You don't need the tie to impress them."

I hesitate, torn between wanting to make a good impression and feeling like an imposter. "Are you sure? I thought..."

She smiles. "I'm sure. Be yourself, remember?"

With relief, I loosen the tie and pull it off, tossing it onto the bed. The simple act of removing it makes me feel less constrained.

"Better?" Zara asks, straightening my collar.

I nod, pulling her close for a quick kiss. "Much better. Thank you, littlefugl."

We walk out of the room and down to the hotel restaurant, my stomach twisting with each step. The place is filled with gleaming silverware and crisp white tablecloths, a far cry from the rustic simplicity of my cabin. I feel like a bull in a china shop, acutely aware of every movement I make.

Zara squeezes my hand as we approach the table. Her parents are already sitting there, waiting.

"Mom, Dad," Zara says warmly, "This is Aksel."

I extend my hand, trying to remember the polite niceties that never came naturally to me. "It's a pleasure to meet you both," I manage, my voice gruffer than intended.

Zara's father shakes my hand firmly, his gaze assessing. Her mother offers a tentative smile.

As we sit down, I'm hyper-aware of my posture, how I hold my hands, and even how I breathe. The waiter approaches with menus, and I realize immediately that I've got no idea how to navigate this world of fine dining.

I sit stiffly in my chair, acutely aware of Frank's scrutinizing gaze. Zara's hand finds mine under the table, her touch grounding me.

Jackie leans forward, her smile warm and genuine. "So, Aksel, Zara tells us you're from Norway. How are you finding Minnesota?"

I clear my throat, grateful for the easy question. "It's different. Flatter. But the people have been welcoming."

Jackie nods enthusiastically. "Oh, we pride ourselves on our hospitality. Glad you've experienced it first hand."

"I have," I respond, my eyes flickering to Zara. She beams at me, and I forget my discomfort for a moment.

Frank's voice cuts through the moment. "And what exactly do you do for a living, Aksel?"

I tense. "I– I'm self-employed. I do freelance work."

Frank's eyebrows raise slightly. "Freelance work? What kind?"

I can feel sweat beading on my forehead. "Mostly consulting. For outdoor expeditions and survival training."

Zara jumps in, her voice bright. "Aksel's an expert in wilderness survival, Dad. You should see his cabin in Norway. It's incredible."

Frank grunts, clearly not impressed. "And how exactly did you two meet? Zara was supposed to be doing research."

I open my mouth to respond, but Jackie interjects. "Frank, don't interrogate the poor man. I'm sure they have a lovely story."

Zara squeezes my hand, taking over. "We met through my research. Aksel was kind enough to let me stay at his place while I conducted my studies."

Frank's eyes narrow. "And now you've quit your job out of the blue? That doesn't sound like you, Zara."

I can feel the tension rising, but before I can speak, the waiter arrives with our drinks. As he sets them down, I catch Frank's gaze. His eyes are hard, protective. I recognize that look because it's the same one I get when protecting what's mine.

Zara's clear and confident voice cuts through the

tension. "Mom and Dad, I quit my job to move to Norway with Aksel."

The silence that follows is deafening. I watch as Frank's face turns a deep shade of red while Jackie's eyes widen in shock. The pit in my stomach grows, and I resist the urge to bare my teeth defensively.

"You what?" Frank sputters, his knuckles white as he grips the table's edge.

Jackie leans forward, her brow furrowed with concern. "Sweetheart, are you sure about this? What about your career? Your research?"

Zara's hand tightens around mine under the table. Her voice remains steady as she responds, "I've given it thought. My work in Norway opened up new possibilities, and Aksel has connections that can help me continue my research independently."

Frank's eyes snap to me, blazing with fury. "Connections? What kind of connections could a wilderness consultant possibly have?"

I clench my jaw, fighting back the growl rising in my throat. Zara speaks before I can, her tone sharp. "Dad, Aksel has resources and knowledge invaluable to my work. This isn't just about him. It's also about what's best for my career and happiness."

Jackie reaches out, placing a hand on Zara's arm. "But honey, Norway is so far away. We'll hardly ever see you."

It's taking every ounce of self-control not to react, to show them exactly why their daughter is safer with me than anyone else. But I know that's not what Zara needs right now.

Instead, I clear my throat and speak up, my voice low but firm. "Mr. and Mrs. Driscoll, I understand your concerns. Zara means everything to me, and I promise you, I'll do whatever it takes to support her dreams and keep her safe."

It's hard to believe those words came out of my mouth. A few weeks ago, before I met Zara, I never would have imagined myself saying anything like that, but I was a different man then. A man consumed by darkness and a thirst for blood. I planned to hunt her and make her prey before ending her life in the wilderness long behind me. It was a sick game I'd played with countless victims, a twisted desire that had consumed me for so long.

But then I met her, and everything changed.

Frank's gaze softens slightly at my words, and I can see him struggling with his protective instincts.

He leans back in his chair, studying me intently. "You say you'll support her dreams," he says. "But how do we know you won't just hold her back? Zara has worked hard to get where she is."

I meet his gaze steadily, refusing to back down. "I would never hold Zara back. Her ambition, her passion for her work—it's one of the things I admire most about her. I want to help her achieve her goals, not hinder them."

Jackie reaches across the table, placing her hand over Zara's. "Sweetheart, we just want you to be happy. If this is what you want and Aksel makes you happy, we'll support you."

Zara's eyes shine with unshed tears as she squeezes her mother's hand. "He does, Mom. He does."

I feel a warmth spreading through my chest at her words. It's a foreign sensation, feeling accepted and part of something other than myself. I've spent so long as a lone wolf that I've forgotten what it's like to belong.

Frank clears his throat, drawing our attention back to him. "Well, Aksel, I can't say I'm thrilled about this. But if Zara trusts you, I'll trust her judgment."

He fixes me with a stern look, his eyes boring into mine. "But let me make one thing clear. If you ever hurt my little girl, if you ever give me a reason to doubt your intentions, there'll be hell to pay. Understood?"

I nod, meeting his gaze without flinching. "Understood, sir. I would never do anything to hurt Zara. She's everything to me."

The words feel strange on my tongue, a confession I never thought I'd make. But as I look at Zara, her eyes shining with love and trust, I know it's true. She's become my whole world, the light that chased away the darkness within me.

Frank nods, seemingly satisfied with my response. Jackie smiles warmly at me, her earlier reservations melting away.

As the waiter arrives to take our orders, I feel a sense of relief wash over me. I know there will be challenges ahead and obstacles to overcome as Zara and I navigate this new path together. But for now, at this moment, I allow myself to bask in the warmth of acceptance, the feeling of finally belonging somewhere.

27

EPILOGUE

ZARA

One year later...

I stand at the summit, the crisp mountain air filling my lungs as I observe the breathtaking view. The snow-capped peaks stretch out before me, a testament to the raw beauty of the Norwegian wilderness. It's hard to believe that a year has passed since I decided to stay with Aksel and pursue my passion for climate research.

With each passing day, my blog has gained more followers, eager to learn about the impact of climate change on this stunning landscape. The data I collect has become invaluable, not only to my readers but also to the Norwegian government. The contract they offered me was a dream come true, validating my hard work and dedication to my research.

As I set up my equipment, my thoughts drift to Aksel.

His unwavering support has been the cornerstone of my success. He's been by my side every step, encouraging me to pursue my dreams and providing security in this wild, untamed land.

The wind whips through my hair as I take the final readings, the numbers on my screen painting a picture of the changing climate. It's a sobering reminder of the importance of my work and the need to raise awareness and inspire action.

I glance up from my data readings, my heart beating harder when I see Aksel emerge from the tree line. He moves with the grace of a predator, his muscles rippling beneath his sweat-soaked shirt. He's wearing one of his camouflage masks, which always excites me. They only add to his dark and rugged appearance. But it's the sight of the dead animal slung over his shoulder that sends a shiver down my spine.

As he draws closer, I can see the blood smeared across his skin, a testament to his prowess as a hunter. The coppery scent fills my nostrils, and I find myself inexplicably drawn to him, like a moth to a flame.

"Successful hunt?" I ask, my voice barely above a whisper.

Aksel grins, his eyes glinting with feral intensity, making my pulse race. "Always, little bird."

He sets the carcass down, and I can't help but stare at how his muscles flex beneath his inked skin. The sight of him, primal and feral, awakens a desire I can barely comprehend.

I shake my head, trying to clear my thoughts. What is

wrong with me? How can I be so turned on by the sight of blood?

But as Aksel steps closer, his scent envelops me, and I lose the battle against my desires. His hand reaches out, brushing a strand of hair from my face, and I lean into his touch, craving more.

"You're thinking about it, aren't you?" Aksel's voice is a low purr.

I swallow, my throat suddenly dry. "Thinking about what?"

His lips curl into a wicked smile, and he steps toward me, closing the distance between us. "You know exactly what I mean, little bird."

I feel a tremor run through me as his scent washes over me, that unique blend of musk and something wilder, more primal. "I—I don't know what you mean."

"Don't you?" He reaches out, his fingers tracing the curve of my neck, sending shivers down my spine. "Your heart is racing. You can't hide how much you want it."

My breath catches in my throat as his hand moves lower, resting on the curve of my hip. "Want what?"

"You know." His lips are inches from my ear, and his breath is hot against my skin. "The edge of the blade. The thrill of it all."

I close my eyes, my body betraying me as a rush of arousal courses through my veins. How does he always know what I'm thinking?

"Say it," he whispers, his fingers tightening around my hip. "Tell me what you want, baby girl."

I open my mouth, but no words come out. I can't bring myself to voice the dark desires that consume me.

Aksel chuckles, his breath tickling my ear. "Don't worry, little bird. I know all your secrets."

Before I can respond, I feel the cold kiss of steel against my skin. I gasp as his knife presses lightly against my throat, a sensation that sends a jolt of excitement through me.

"Shall we play, baby girl?" His voice is a silky murmur, his eyes glittering with anticipation.

I swallow, my pulse thrumming in my veins. "Yes."

The word is barely a whisper, but it's enough. In one swift motion, he spins me around, pressing me against his chest. I feel the knife leave my throat, only to return a moment later, slicing lightly across my shoulder.

The pain is sharp but fleeting, quickly replaced by a surge of pleasure as Aksel leans down, his tongue tracing the path of the blade, tasting my blood.

I moan, my head falling back against his shoulder as he continues his devilish ministrations. His free hand roams my body, stoking the flames of my desire.

"That's it. Let me hear you."

I cry out, my body arching into his touch as he nips at my shoulder, marking me with his mouth. The knife, the blood, his intimate touches—they blur together, creating a symphony of sensations that push me closer and closer to the edge.

"Please..." I don't realize I've spoken the word until I hear it hanging in the air between us.

"Please, what?" He murmurs, his lips brushing my ear.

"Please, Aksel. I need you."

He smirks, and I feel a shiver run down my spine. With a swift movement, he withdraws the blade and steps back.

"Run, little bird. Make me work for it."

My heart pounds in my chest, and I turn and dash into the trees without another thought. The cool air whips against my skin, sending goosebumps along my arms. I can hear Aksel following behind me.

I dodge between the trees, their branches reaching out like gnarled fingers. The earth is soft and muddy beneath my feet, threatening to slow my progress, but I push on, driven by the thrill of the chase.

I leave my equipment behind in haste, but I know it'll be safe. No one dares to venture into Aksel's territory uninvited.

My breath comes in short gasps as I run, the familiar landscape guiding my path. I aim for the waterfall halfway back to the cabin, hoping to reach it before Aksel catches me. The thought of him taking me against the rocky cliff, the sound of the water echoing around us, sends a thrill through my body.

The rush of the waterfall grows louder as I draw closer, the mist cooling my heated skin. I spot the shimmering curtain of water through the trees and know I'm almost there.

I scramble over the rocky terrain, my heart pounding in my chest. With one final surge of speed, I burst into the clearing behind the water, the powerful spray soaking my skin.

I spin around, my chest heaving as I search for Aksel.

The sound of his approaching footsteps comes to a halt, and I know he has spotted me behind the curtain of water.

Slowly, he steps into the clearing, his eyes dark and hungry. Water droplets catch in his eyelashes.

Without a word, he begins to stalk toward me, moving with the deliberate grace of a predator. My heart is pounding in my chest, a mixture of excitement and anticipation coursing through my veins as I back up against the rocky wall behind me.

He reaches out, his fingers grazing my cheek, and pulls me roughly against his chest. I can feel his heart thundering against mine, the rhythm of our desire syncopating in the air between us.

His mouth crushes mine in a feverish kiss, his tongue demanding entrance. I moan, opening to him, our passion igniting like a flame in the crisp mountain air.

The force of his kiss pushes me back against the rock face, the cold stone a stark contrast to the heat of his body. Aksel's hands move urgently over me, sliding under my shirt to grasp my breasts, his thumbs circling my nipples with just the right amount of pressure.

I moan into his mouth, my hands tangling in his hair as I pull him closer, desperate for more. He tears his mouth from mine, his lips trailing down my neck, leaving a trail of hot, open-mouthed kisses that make my head spin.

"You like that, baby girl?" he growls, his breath hot against my skin.

"God, yes," I gasp, my body aching for him.

With a rough tug, he rips open the buttons of my

flannel shirt, the cool air hitting my skin and causing my nipples to tighten. He takes one peak into his mouth, sucking and nibbling until I'm squirming against him, my hands gripping his biceps.

"What do you want, little bird?" He pulls back to look at me, his eyes dark with desire. "Tell me what you need."

I bite my lip, not wanting to voice my deepest desires but unable to deny my need for him. "I need you," I whisper, my voice hoarse with want. "Give me your cock, Aksel. Please."

A primal growl rumbles in his chest as he scoops me up, pressing me back against the rock with my legs wrapped around his waist. The hard length of him presses against me through the fabric of his jeans, and I whimper, needing to feel him inside me.

He unzips his pants and pulls his dick out, making me moan when I feel it slap against my clit. "Do you want me to claim this sweet pussy, baby girl?" He teases my entrance with the tip of his cock, making me cry out with need.

"Yes! Oh God! Yes!"

With one swift thrust, he buries himself inside me, filling me. My head falls back as pleasure rocks through me. His hands grasp my hips, holding me in place as he moves with deep and powerful thrusts.

"That's it, little bird. Take it all." He pulls out until just the tip is inside, then slams back into me, again and again, each thrust hitting my sweet spot.

I can feel the rough rock grazing my back. The waterfall

echoes around us, blending with my moans as Aksel drives me higher.

"You like getting fucked out here in the wild, don't you, baby girl?" He leans down, his mouth at my ear as he continues to thrust into me. "You like the idea of someone stumbling upon us, seeing me claim you like the animal you are?"

His words spark a fire in my belly, something wild and untamed. "Yes! fuck, yes!"

He chuckles, his breath hot against my skin. "That's it, let it out. Scream for me."

I cry out, my nails digging into his back as he pounds into me, his hips slapping against my ass. The pleasure builds, a coiling tension deep in my core that threatens to consume me.

"Come for me, littlefugl. Let me feel you tighten around my cock." His voice is a guttural demand, his thrusts becoming more urgent.

His words send me over the edge, and I cry out as my orgasm rips through me. My body shakes uncontrollably as waves of pleasure wash over me, my inner walls clenching tightly around him.

Aksel groans, his grip on my hips tightening as he finds his release. "Fuck, baby, you feel so good. I'm not going to last much longer."

I tighten my legs around him, wanting to feel him spill his cum deep inside me. "Come for me, Aksel. Breed me."

With a few more powerful thrusts, he roars, his body shuddering as he spills himself into me. He buries his face in my neck, his breath coming in sharp gasps as he rides out his release.

Slowly, he slides out of me, and I whimper at the loss, my body still humming with pleasure. He yanks me against his chest, holding me close.

I feel his heart slowing, his breath evening out against my skin. "That was—"

"Incredible," we finish together, laughing softly.

He nuzzles my neck, his lips pressing soft kisses along my skin. "I love you, little bird."

"I love you too, Aksel." I tilt my head back, offering my mouth to his.

As his lips capture mine, I know that no matter what the future holds, I would never trade this—the wildness of the Norwegian wilderness, the thrill of discovery in my research, and the unfathomable depths of my love for this man.

* * *

THANK YOU FOR READING *Hunted!* Did you enjoy it? If so check out my other books, including Carnival Nightmare which is the first in an interconnected world of books set around a traveling carnival.

Carnival Nightmare is a dark & spicy 48k word dark romance featuring a hot, tattooed psychopath who becomes instantly obsessed with the FMC the moment he sees her.

Grab your copy here: Carnival Nightmare: A Dark Stalker Romance

More books by me:
Carnival Monster: A Dark Serial Killer Romance
Welcome to Carnage: A Dark Romance novella
Salvation: A Dark Stalker Romance
Stranded: A Dark Romance novella
Carjacked: A Dark Hitchhiker Romance

ABOUT THE AUTHOR

I've always been drawn to the dark side of fiction. My stories? They're an exploration of that darkness, filled with mysterious masked men, fearless heroines, and spice that'll set your Kindles ablaze.

Ever since I can remember, I've been captivated by the darker side of romance. It's necessary to add I don't condone these kind of relationships in real life. However, the intoxicating chase, the deadly dance, the heart-racing fear, and an irresistible attraction I adore writing.

I exclusively publish on Amazon, providing a thrilling escape for those who dare to venture into the dark side of love and lust. If you've read my book and found yourself wanting more, follow me on Amazon or social media for updates on my next dark novella release. Your adventure is only a page flip away.

ALSO BY THIS AUTHOR

Welcome to Carnage: A Dark Romance novella
Stranded: A Dark Romance novella
Salvation: A Dark Stalker Romance
Carjacked: A Dark Hitchhiker Romance
Carnival Nightmare: A Dark Stalker Romance
Carnival Monster: A Dark Serial Killer Romance

Printed in Great Britain
by Amazon